Pancakes and Potions

Witch Haven Cozy Mystery - book 6

K.E. O'Connor

K.E. O'Connor Books

While every precaution has been taken in the preparation of this book, the publisher assumes no responsibility for errors or omissions, or for damages resulting from the use of the information contained herein.

All rights reserved.

No portion of this book may be reproduced in any form without written permission from the publisher or author, except as permitted by U.S. copyright law.

PANCAKES AND POTIONS

Copyright © 2022 by K.E. O'Connor

ISBN: 978-1-915378-33-0

Written by: K.E. O'Connor

Preface

The Witch Haven series has been created so you spend time with four amazing witches:

Books 1-3 tell Indigo's story: Spells and Spooks, Hexes and Haunts, Curses and Corpses

Books 4-6 tell Luna's story: Muffins and Moonlight, Cupcakes and Cauldrons, Pancakes and Potions

Book 7-9 tell Odessa's story: Hauntings and High Jinx, Hauntings and Havoc, Hauntings and Hoaxes

Book 10-12 tell Storm's story: The Case of the Screaming Skull, The Case of the Poisoned Pumpkin, The Case of the Cursed Candy

And there are two bonus origin stories to enjoy: **Fire Fang** and **Silvaria**

Chapter 1

I paced the corridor in the hospital for what felt like the thousandth time. Only Cole standing in front of me and blocking my path stopped me from wearing holes in my boots.

He gently cupped my face and wiped the tears off my cheeks with his thumbs. "Your uncle will be okay. They got him out in time."

"You don't know that. And what's taking them so long? He could have serious burns or damage to his lungs because of smoke inhalation. I need to see him. I should be in there with him." My breath came out ragged, my head hurting from so much crying.

"The doctors know what they're doing. And you need looking at, too." Cole lifted the ends of my hair, which were frazzled from the intense heat of the fire at Fandango's.

"I didn't get hurt. You were there to protect me." I slumped against him and wrapped my arms around his waist.

He hissed out a breath, and it was only when my hands slid down his back that I realized part of his shirt was shredded.

Cole gently eased away my hands and settled them on his butt. "Go easy with the tight hugs until my back heals."

"You should have told me you were injured." I hurried around behind him. Bright pink skin showed beneath the tattered shirt.

"You know me. A werewolf can heal from almost anything. I'm more worried about you."

"Are you sure? We can get a nurse to see you." I skimmed my fingers lightly over his hot flesh, so grateful for the power of werewolf magic.

"Positive. They don't need to waste their healing energy on my burns. I'll be fine in the morning."

I leaned against his solid chest. I breathed in the scent of smoke, burned cloth, and spicy Cole.

"What do you think happened at the bakery?" His voice was soft under the bright lights of the hospital waiting room.

"I have no idea. We get the equipment regularly serviced, but maybe something malfunctioned. We have a lot of things that could catch fire." I shook my head. "But Uncle Albert is always so careful about shutting things down. He never leaves anything on. And I know I didn't."

"This has nothing to do with you. We were out for most of the day."

I sighed. "I really want to talk to Uncle Albert. Maybe he saw something."

"Luna!"

At the sound of Indigo Ash's voice, I turned. Right behind her were my two other closest friends, Storm Winter and Odessa Grimsbane. Cole stepped back as all three of them engulfed me in hugs, and in seconds, we were talking over each other. Odessa and Indigo were crying, and even Storm's eyes looked hazy, and she rarely shed a tear.

"How's your uncle doing?" Indigo pulled back from the hug.

"I haven't seen him yet. That can't be a good sign."

Cole's hand rested on my shoulder. "It's a sign the doctors are working hard. They'll let you in soon."

"What happened at the bakery?" Storm's dark hair was scraped off her face in a messy ponytail. "I heard the explosion from my apartment."

I stepped back and rubbed a hand across my face. "I don't know. It all happened so fast, my brain hasn't caught up. I was outside with Cole when the fire appeared out of nowhere."

"Oh! You're lucky to still be standing if you were that close to the flames." Odessa gripped me tight, her round cheeks pink and her eyes full of concern.

"I had someone watching my back." I smiled at Cole before focusing on Storm. "Are you sure about the explosion?"

"It sounded like it. The air was sucked out of my place, and then there was a boom. It took me a few minutes to figure out what was going on. Fire Fang alerted me to the problem. He kept pacing around the apartment and whining. I took him out to take a look, and we discovered Fandango's on fire."

"You must have just missed us. The fire crew found Uncle Albert quickly, and we came in the ambulance." I rubbed my aching forehead. "We have nothing explosive in the bakery. I figured maybe an electrical fire, but I don't know..."

"Do you think magic caused the explosion?" Indigo said.

My friends exchanged a worried glance.

"I... maybe. I hadn't thought."

"Who would do that to you?" Storm said.

Indigo ducked her head. "I was thinking my mom and her freaky boyfriend could be back."

"I can't think about the cause." I caught hold of Indigo's hand. "But it's not your mom. She's gone. All I care about right now is Uncle Albert and making sure he's fine. I'll figure out the rest later."

"We'll stay here until you know how he's doing," Odessa said.

I sucked in a shaky breath, my heart giving a desperately unhappy thud. "Actually, I need help with something else. Earl. They couldn't find him in the bakery. The firefighters were putting out the blaze, but I had to leave with Uncle Albert. I... I think Earl's dead."

Cole's hand tightened on my shoulder.

"We can go look for him," Odessa said. "Would you like us to do that?"

I swallowed. "I have to know what happened to him, but it won't be safe at the bakery. The firefighters wouldn't let me anywhere near the building, even though I begged them to let me find him. They were having trouble controlling the blaze."

"Not anymore. The fire's out," Storm said. "Haven't you checked outside? It's raining buckets."

I glanced at the window and only then noticed the torrential rain pounding the glass. I'd never been so happy to see a rainstorm in my life.

"We can find Earl." Odessa squeezed my hand. "You know him, he always tucks himself away. I expect he was protected on top of a cupboard or inside a mixing bowl out of the way of any trouble."

"I hope so." I could barely get the words out. Earl wasn't the greatest familiar in the world, but I couldn't imagine him not being in my life. He was my adorable, lazy furball, and I had to find him.

"We'll get him. You'll be fine and so will your uncle," Indigo said. "Then we'll figure out what happened at the bakery."

The main doors slammed open. Zek, one of the teenage gremlins I was teaching at the reform school, staggered through the doors clutching something black and smoking. Trotting beside him was Fire Fang, who growled at anyone who got too close.

Zek dropped to his knees and wheezed out a breath. "I need help here. I have an injured familiar."

My eyes widened as I took in what he was holding. "Is that Earl?"

Zek looked up at me. "Yeah. I saved him for you."

I raced over, almost colliding with a nurse as she stopped and peered at Earl.

"Oh! I thought that was a baby. It's just an animal," she said.

"He's more than that. He's my familiar." My hands shook as I touched Earl. "And he's been in a fire. He needs medical treatment."

"Then he needs to go to the vet. We don't treat animals here."

I rounded on her. "You'll treat him. And Zek."

Zek lifted a hand. "I'm good. Just got messed up from the smoke."

The nurse pursed her lips, a shimmer of indecision in her eyes. "Maybe some pain relief, but the vet is the specialist for familiars." She strode away.

I gently rested a hand on Earl's side, relieved to feel him breathing. I gripped Zek's shoulder. "How did you find him?"

"We heard about the fire at the reform school and went to look. We were worried about you. You're our least worst teacher, so we didn't want you getting crispy around the edges." He gave me a sharp-toothed grin. "When the firefighters pulled back, one of the others said he heard a noise inside. The guys distracted the firefighters, and I crept in. I found this little dude and remembered you saying you had a black cat familiar."

I wrapped my arms around Zek, being careful not to squash Earl, and hugged him tight. "Thank you. I thought I'd lost him."

"No worries. You saved me from choking to death on a cupcake. It's only right I repay the debt. I always do."

More tears slid down my cheeks. "You're incredible. I don't know how I'll ever thank you."

"No need. I owed you, and now we're even. Although if you give me a couple of extra marks on my next assessment, I wouldn't mind."

I smiled at him as I carefully stroked Earl. I couldn't see any burns, but his eyes were closed, and he didn't respond, no matter how many times I said his name.

Fire Fang nudged me out of the way with his enormous head and wiped his huge pink tongue across Earl. He did it several times, occasionally pausing to spit out black bits of charred fur he'd scraped off.

"Is that a good idea?" I inched away as Fire Fang growled at me.

Storm nudged me. "He knows what he's doing. There's more to that hellhound mutt than meets the eye. He knows things. It's freaky. And he's still levitating when he sleeps."

Earl made a hacking cough, and his eyes flew open. Fire Fang backed away and lowered himself to the floor, giving a gentle whine.

"Earl, can you hear me?" I knelt in front of him.

He coughed up a huge ball of gross looking black goo and slow blinked at me. "Am I dead?"

"You came close. Zek rescued you from Fandango's. Do you remember anything about how the fire started?"

Earl looked at Zek. "Huh! You saved me?"

Zek puffed out his chest. "Yeah. I found you wedged in a dented tin. You were under a table at the back of the bakery."

"How did I get there?" Earl uncurled himself and inspected each paw. "I was taking a nap in my favorite brownie tin under the counter when there was a bang. That's all I remember. I wasn't under a table when I dozed off."

"Do you know where the bang came from?" I said.

Earl flopped out of Zek's arms and dropped to the floor. He shook himself and sniffed his fur. His nose wrinkled. "Maybe the kitchen. I don't know.

It happened fast. I was sleeping, there was a noise, and that was it."

"Whatever it was, it must have been violent enough to propel you across the bakery," Indigo said.

Earl nodded. His head shot up. "What about Albert? He was upstairs after he'd shut the bakery for the night."

"We're still waiting to find out," I said.

Zek stood and brushed down his soot covered clothing. "I'll leave you to it."

I hugged him again. "You're my hero. You were so brave."

He pulled back and grinned. "Make sure that goes down on my assessment. Maybe I'll get out of the reform school early for such heroic behavior."

"I'll make sure it does. I'll see you in class soon."

He nodded at me and strode away, his chest puffed up and a swagger in his step.

The nurse returned. "I'll look at your familiar now."

"Nope. No need for any medical probing. I'm okay," Earl said. "I feel good. Although I smell weird. I could do with a bath, and I don't say that often."

"Luna Brimstone?" A middle-aged doctor in a white coat appeared in the waiting room.

"That's me." I raced over.

His smile was reassuring as he nodded at me. "I've been with your uncle. He's going to be fine."

A huge weight lifted off my shoulders when I heard those words. "Thank you. Can I see him?"

"Yes. He's awake and talking, but he's going to need rest. And he got burned. Healing spells have already been applied, but we want to monitor him for smoke damage and shock."

"Of course. So long as I can see him."

"Just for a few minutes. And only you." His gaze cut to everyone lurking behind me.

I looked back at my amazing group of friends, and they waved me away.

"Go. We'll be here when you come out," Indigo said.

I hurried along with the doctor and into a quiet room along the corridor.

Uncle Albert was sitting up in bed. I sucked in a breath. He looked so small and pale tucked under pristine white sheets. Both his hands were wrapped in thick bandages and a pale pink glow shimmered around them.

I hurried to his bed, determined not to burst into tears and worry him.

"Five minutes," the doctor said from the doorway. "Then he needs to rest for the night. So do you. It must've been a shock seeing what happened to your business."

I nodded, but my attention was on Uncle Albert. I went to grab his hand but pulled back, not wanting to hurt him. "I'm not sure where's safe to touch."

His smile was wobbly. "It's best not to grab my hands. I got burned moving things. I was upstairs when the fire started, and I made it down the stairs, but hot metal blocked the way."

Tears filled my eyes. "How are you feeling?"

"Numb and giggly. I have amazing healing magic pulsing through me. I'm sure I won't feel this good tomorrow when it's worn off. How about you? And Earl?"

"Earl's okay. Someone found him. He's in the waiting room. I was outside the bakery with Cole when the fire started." I pressed a hand against his arm. "I couldn't get to you. The flames were so intense. They came out of nowhere."

He nodded. "One minute, I was snoozing in my easy chair listening to the radio, and the next, there was a bang and smoke poured into the room. The flames moved so quickly."

"I'm so glad you got out in one piece." I looked at the bandages and bit my lip. "Your poor hands."

He sighed. "I won't be able to do any baking for a while. How bad is the damage to Fandango's? Do we still have a business?"

"I didn't wait around to see. I came straight to the hospital with you." My bottom lip jutted out. "But the flames were already out the roof as we left. I'm not sure we can save it."

His gaze lowered, and his shoulders sank. "Oh, well, I was thinking the place needed a makeover. Now, I've got no excuse. Although this will be more than new tables and chairs and a coat of paint. Perhaps we can come up with the new design together. This could be a fresh start."

Uncle Albert always looked on the bright side of things, no matter how grim it got. "It'll get the best makeover."

He nodded. "And we're insured, so we don't have to worry about the money. But if it's as bad as you think, it'll take a long time to rebuild. We'll be out of business for months."

"Don't worry about that. We'll figure something out. You concentrate on healing. We need to make sure your hands are able to knead that magic dough. Otherwise, customers will complain."

His gaze ran over me. He opened his mouth as if he was going to say something then simply nodded. "You're right. There's no rush. Are you sure you weren't hurt?"

"Cole protected me. His back got burned, but he's already healing."

"Then thank him for me. He's a good man. I trust him with you."

"I trust him with me, too. Cole's always looking out for me."

"When I'm up to it, I'll make him a thank you meal. And it's time I got to know him better if things are serious between you." He tilted his head. "Are they serious?"

"Cole would love that." I smoothed his sheets. "And things are moving in the right direction, although we're still getting to know each other. We had a great date today."

The doctor returned. "Your uncle needs to rest. You can come back and see him in the morning."

I kissed Uncle Albert's cheek. "Make sure you get plenty of sleep. I'll be back first thing."

"You rest, too. And don't worry about me. I'm in the best place. The doctors here are amazing."

After giving him a careful hug, I left his room and gently closed the door behind me. It was only then I realized I had nowhere to sleep. My home was gone. Where was I supposed to go?

Chapter 2

"Does anyone want more pumpkin spiced pancakes?" Odessa stood by her large oak kitchen table, an apron with a huge smiling pumpkin face on it tied around her middle. She held aloft a plate stacked with pancakes.

I patted my stomach and shook my head. "I'm stuffed. Thanks. They were amazing."

Cole sat next to me. "I could take another stack of pancakes. Healing burns uses up a ton of calories."

"Coming right up." Odessa filled his plate then poured more coffee for us all before sitting opposite me with her own stack of pancakes.

She'd been amazing last night and instantly offered rooms in her sprawling farmhouse when I'd returned from seeing Uncle Albert. Odessa lived alone, if you didn't count her scarecrows, and had plenty of space. But even if she'd lived in a cramped one-bed apartment, she'd have offered the couch. It was just the way Odessa was. She was a nurturer and an amazing friend.

Cole had also stayed last night. He'd slept in his own room, but I'd taken comfort knowing he was just on the other side of the wall if I needed him.

Odessa grabbed a shaker of her favorite dried pumpkin blend and sprinkled it over her breakfast pancakes. "You can take some pancakes to Albert when you see him today."

"I'm sure he'd love them. He's a food snob, so I doubt the hospital breakfast will be up to his usual standards." I lifted a hand and gently tickled Earl's head. He was wrapped around my neck, fast asleep. He smelled much sweeter after I'd given him a late-night bath. And he'd barely complained as I'd washed away the smoky stench, hellhound spit, and soot.

"Was the bed comfortable?" Odessa asked.

"Perfect. I didn't want to get out of it this morning. Neither did Earl."

"I'm glad you both slept so well," Odessa said. "Shock does strange things to people. Some get wiped out, and others can't sleep for days."

"I think your amazingly comfy bed helped me to unwind."

She grinned. "I aim to please. And you're welcome to stay as long as you like. All of you."

Cole nodded. "I appreciate that. I'm glad to be here so I can help Luna with whatever she needs."

I reached over and squeezed his hand. "Me, too."

I sat back and sipped my coffee while they ate breakfast. Since the shock of the fire was fading, logic was clicking into place. And along with it, a healthy dose of anger. That fire hadn't been an accident, and I had a good idea who was behind it.

"Are you going to see the Fire Chief today?" Odessa said. "Mitchell could have news about Fandango's."

"That's the plan. And I thought I'd head over there this morning. I want to see how bad the site is. Uncle Albert is worried it'll need to be rebuilt."

Odessa's expression turned sympathetic. "Don't expect too much. That fire was raging when I arrived. If it hadn't been for the crazy amount of rain last night, there'd be nothing left. And probably the buildings on either side would have gone up, too."

I looked out the window at the heavy gray clouds. "It looks like we've got more rain coming. Maybe that's a good thing. It'll wash away some of the damage."

"Did your uncle say what plans he has for the site, or is it too soon to think about it?" Odessa said.

"As always, he was amazing. He said he was thinking about having a makeover, anyway, so the fire has kicked him into action."

"That'll be one epic makeover." Odessa glugged down coffee. "I wondered if he might retire. Starting from scratch will be a huge undertaking."

"He always planned to hand the business to me." I shuddered at the thought of keeping the bakery going on my own. "But it might be time for him to hang up his apron and enjoy his golden years. I don't want him working himself into an early grave."

"Your uncle loves baking," Odessa said. "What would he do if he doesn't bake?"

I shrugged. "There's more to life than baking."

Her gaze turned curious. "If you say so."

"We won't make any plans until I've seen the site and figured out how much it'll cost to put back together." I glanced at Cole. "Are you free today? Want to come with me?"

"I'd love to. I've got local pack business to deal with, though." He leaned against me. "I'll call Atticus and rearrange. The wolves will just have to bicker among themselves."

"No, that's fine. I don't want to get in the way of werewolf drama. I was just going to drop by the bakery and then spend the day with Uncle Albert at the hospital. You'd get bored hanging around with me."

He lifted my hand and kissed the back of it. "That would be impossible. And I like spending time with your uncle. He's a good guy."

"He thinks the same about you. He's already invited you to dinner once his hands are healed."

"That sounds good to me. I never turn down great company and a good meal."

Odessa sighed. "You two are so adorable."

I smiled at her. I never thought I'd fall for a werewolf, but Cole and I had been through a lot in a short amount of time. That had bonded us. It would be weird not having him in my life.

"It's just you and me, Earl." I leaned my head against him.

He grumbled and squeezed himself tighter around my neck. He'd been quiet all night, sleeping on my pillow right by my head, which was unusual. Earl usually slept alone. He must have been rattled after everything that happened.

"I've been thinking about the fire," Cole said. "If it was an electrical fault, it would have started in one place and then spread."

"That sounds right," Odessa said. "Do you think that's what happened?"

"Let's not worry about it now. None of us are fire experts." I had my own ideas about how the fire got started, but I wasn't ready to share.

"We were right outside the bakery, and that fire went from zero to a thousand in only a few seconds. Storm and Earl mentioned hearing a bang. I couldn't hear anything for a few seconds after the fire started, so whatever it was, it was so loud it messed with my hearing. It was intense and fast," Cole said.

"Which means?" Odessa said.

"It means nothing. We should wait to see what Mitchell has to say once they've investigated the site." I stood. "Does anyone want more coffee?"

Odessa pointed at the pot. "Help yourself."

"I'm thinking it might not have been an accident." Cole's gaze flickered amber as he watched me.

Odessa gasped. "You can't think Albert started the fire deliberately."

"No. This wasn't Albert's doing. But what if someone else is involved?" Cole's look was pointed as he remained focused on me.

I turned away and concentrated on the job of coffee replenishing. "Who would want to set fire to Fandango's? People drive miles for our food."

"If someone did this deliberately, they must be a monster. It's cruel to deprive the village of Albert's amazing treats. And yours, of course, Luna," Odessa said.

I rolled my eyes. "Sure. My desserts are perfection." There was one small bright side to this mess. I wouldn't have to fake my natural baking talents. With Fandango's out of commission, no one would notice me producing stale scones or a cheesecake that tasted of boiled socks.

"It's just a theory," Cole said. "But that was an intense blaze. We shouldn't rule out arson."

"I'm not ruling anything in or out," I said. "It's too soon to prove anything."

Odessa caught hold of my hand as I returned to the table. "If someone did this to Fandango's, you're welcome to use my scarecrows to get revenge. My boys love whipping butt, and they always have excess energy to burn off, so hunting a bad guy would be a treat for them."

"Thanks. I might take you up on that. But we don't need to get ahead of ourselves." I looked out the window. "I'll just grab some air. You two finish breakfast."

"Is everything okay?" Cole said. "I didn't mean to worry you with the arson theory."

I kissed his cheek. "I'm fine. I've just got a lot to think about." I left them to their food and headed outside with Earl still wrapped around me like a big black fur stole.

I leaned against the front porch, and a light drizzle drifted down around me. "Earl, I'm really sorry."

He wriggled around. "What are you sorry for?"

"You should have been with me. I sometimes don't think about you. I... I should be a better witch to you." I kept my gaze on the horizon.

He was silent for several seconds. "Ain't that the truth."

"If you'd been with me yesterday, you wouldn't have gotten hurt. Most witches spend more time with their familiars."

"True. I'm surprised you even care what happened to me."

"Hey! I care. We don't have the strongest witch and familiar bond, but I still don't want anything bad to happen to you."

"If I'd died in that fire, you'd be free of me."

I lifted Earl gently and turned him so I could see him. "That's not a nice thing to say. I don't want to get rid of you."

His ears flattened. "So you say."

The bitterness in his tone shocked me. "That's what you really think? I don't want you around?"

"What else am I supposed to think? You never make use of me. Other witches have their familiars around most of the time. Indigo only has to click her fingers and her three familiars are there for her."

"Not always Nugget."

"Nugget is there when it matters. You can guarantee that creepy spider is close by, and Russell is always fluttering overhead. That's a true familiar bond in action. And Storm's always got Fire Fang lurking about."

"I'm not sure she has much choice. Fire Fang goes where he wants to. And she's adamant he's not her familiar."

"They belong to each other. They're the perfect fit. Both darkly terrifying and take no nonsense from anyone."

"Do you think we don't belong to each other?"

"We get on okay, when you remember I'm here."

"I know you're always around." I bit my lip. "But you never seem interested in what I do. I always think I'm bothering you."

"Because baking bores me. And I know it does you. You don't like doing it. Making cakes sucks."

"I've never said that."

"You don't have to. Your actions speak volumes. And you only stay at the bakery because of Albert. I love the old guy, but doing something every day that sets your teeth on edge affects me, too. Your mood is my mood."

"I... maybe I do stay for Uncle Albert. What else am I supposed to do? Leave him to run the business singlehandedly?"

Earl jumped out of my arms and landed on the porch railing. "Talk to him. You always do a great job of pretending everything is fine. You're not fine, and neither am I. I know the thought of spending the rest of your life baking makes you sick. And I don't want to spend my life being a witch's familiar and having no purpose. Baking isn't for us. It's not what you do, and it's not what I want to do. All that flour makes me sneeze. And don't get me started on how gross all those herbs are." He poked out a pink tongue.

My heart thudded. I couldn't leave this behind. I had nothing else. "It's what I'm supposed to do. I'm a Brimstone baker. Baking magic runs through our blood."

Earl shook out his fur and did a full body stretch, arching his spine and flicking his tail. "Then we need to renegotiate this arrangement."

"You want to separate from me? I'd have no familiar if you left."

"You'd find a better one. Or do without. Not every witch has a familiar. Odessa doesn't."

"She has her scarecrows. They're her surrogate familiars." I shook my head. "It would be wrong not to have you around. Where would you go?"

His nose wrinkled, and he turned away from me. "It would have been better if I hadn't made it out of the fire. Then we wouldn't be stuck with each other."

My throat tightened. "You'd be happier dead than living with me?"

Earl still didn't look at me. "You barely make use of me. I'm an annoyance."

I swallowed around the lump in my throat. I had neglected him. Witches gained strength from their familiars. They enhanced their natural powers and supported them, but my baking powers had never worked properly. Earl had seen time and again how they failed and how I fudged my ability so no one saw what a fraud I was. And all this time, I'd been misusing him by doing that.

Cole stepped out onto the porch. "How are you doing?"

I glanced at Earl. "We're good. We will be, anyway."

Cole wrapped his arms around me from behind and pressed me against his chest. "I really don't want to leave you. I'll tell Atticus to deal with things on his own."

"The werewolves need you. I have my friends looking out for me. And I have Earl. Besides, I won't be doing anything exciting. We can meet for dinner. Odessa's a great cook, and she always makes huge portions."

"If you're sure."

"I am."

"Then I'll look forward to seeing you at dinner." He gave me a sweet kiss on my forehead. "Just so you know, I'm also here to protect you. You can look after yourself, but you have me, too. And I'm not going anywhere."

"Thanks. I appreciate it."

After seeing Cole off, I grabbed my purse, said goodbye to Odessa, and left the farmhouse. I stopped at the bottom of the steps and looked back at Earl. "Do you want to come with me?"

"I'm staying here. I'll only get in the way."

I sighed. I had a lot of work to do to get my familiar back on side. Maybe I was already too late, and the relationship was too damaged to repair.

As I reached the end of the driveway, I frowned, and my stomach flipped. Devlin Goody was marching toward me. That was the last thing I needed. Devlin was an overly officious employee of the Magic Council, always quick to blame me for everything, and usually in the wrong when solving crimes.

I strode toward him. "I can't stop."

"I'll walk with you." He adjusted the wide-brimmed black hat on his head.

"There's no need. I'm not great company."

"There's every need."

I stopped and turned to him. "Not now! My uncle is in the hospital."

He stood his ground, although his face paled. "I'm sorry about your uncle, but Fandango's was burned to the ground last night, and I don't think it was an accident."

Chapter 3

I grabbed Devlin's arm so hard he squeaked. "If you think I had anything to do with the fire that almost killed my uncle and my familiar, we're falling out."

He glared down at my hand clamped around his arm. "It seems suspicious that I'm investigating the bakery—"

"You're not! There's nothing to investigate."

Devlin finally extracted his arm from my grip. "There's still an open investigation regarding the strange magic you use in your food. That hasn't gone away."

"It should. You won't find anything." I jabbed a finger at him. "Go deal with real criminals and leave me alone. I need to focus on my family." I turned and strode along the road, heading to the hospital.

Devlin raced along beside me. "Luna, your magic is strange. You've even admitted that it sometimes doesn't work how you expect it to work. I'm simply investigating all possibilities."

I slid him a glare as I kept marching. "And what possibilities have you unearthed this time? I suppose you're going to say I blew up the bakery because I don't like baking cakes. Or I'm hiding evidence that I'm a secret serial killer."

He was silent for a few seconds. "They're possibilities. Maybe not the serial killer part. You don't fit the profile."

"Go away, Devlin. I can't deal with you and your poorly formed opinion of me. I might not be the best baker in the world, but I love my family. I'd never set fire to Fandango's with Uncle Albert and Earl inside. If you really think that, then you know nothing about me." Angry tears sprang into my eyes, but I swiped them away before they could fall.

He puffed along beside me. "The initial findings from the Fire Chief show this wasn't an accident."

"I'm going to see Mitchell. I'll find out everything I need to then."

"I... I could tell you the preliminary findings, if you're interested."

My glare would have soured milk. "Why bother? You think I've done it, so I should already know everything."

He sighed. "Perhaps I was a little abrupt with you."

"Do you think? Every time we meet, you accuse me of crimes I didn't commit. You should have learned your lesson by now. I'm not a killer. And I love my family." I was walking so fast my breath was rasping out of me, but I wasn't slowing down to spend any more time with Devlin than necessary.

He kept up the frantic pace as we drew closer to the hospital. "Mitchell found evidence of a concentrated blast of magic in the kitchen."

I looked at him. "Magic? It wasn't an electrical fault?"

Devlin shook his head as he took off his hat and wiped his forehead with a handkerchief. "Electrical faults have been discounted. Someone blew up your bakery."

I gritted my teeth. I knew exactly who that someone was. I had Bram Vexx, an unhappy debt collector, on my back, and it looked like he'd returned to get revenge because I hadn't paid what I owed.

"Have you any idea who'd want to destroy Fandango's?"

I hesitated. Should I tell Devlin about my financial problems? The last time he found me in trouble with Bram Vexx, he let him get away with robbing the bakery.

Devlin replaced his hat. "I know we haven't always gotten along, but I'm here to uphold magical law. If you know anything that can help solve this crime, you need to let me know."

I shook my head. "I can't focus on the bakery right now. I'm going to see Uncle Albert."

He opened his mouth as if to say more and then nodded. "I'll stop by and see your uncle later today. Perhaps he has some useful information."

"Speak to him but don't put Uncle Albert under any pressure while he's recovering." I dashed away without waiting for a response. Bram would pay for what he'd done to Fandango's. And I'd be the one to exact that revenge.

I hurried through the main doors of the hospital and stop dead. My mom, Cloris Brimstone, stood by the visitors' chairs in a fitted black pantsuit with a red scarf tied around her slim throat.

She lifted her head as if she sensed me watching. "Luna!"

I unstuck my feet from the floor and dashed over to hug her. "What are you doing here? You're supposed to be in Bermuda, baking for some prince, aren't you?"

Her hug was tight as the scent of freshly baked chocolate chip cookies enveloped me. It was my mom's unique scent. Her magic was always so powerful it made my nose tickle. "I got a call about Albert. I dropped everything and came to see how he was. The prince will have to wait for his desserts."

I pulled back from our hug and stared at my mom. I hadn't seen her in over a year. She had an elegant grace about her, with perfectly styled brunette hair in a neat bob. Her dark eyes had a few more wrinkles around them than mine, but I definitely took after my mom for looks.

She smiled and tucked a piece of loose hair behind my ear. "How are you? Albert said you were outside the bakery when it caught fire."

"I was. But I wasn't hurt. I really can't believe you're here. It's been ages."

"I had to come." She tugged the hem of my orange flower print tunic. "Is this designer?"

I brushed her hand away. "No. How long are you staying?"

"At least a week. Everything has been arranged with my work, and my employer was understanding."

"Luna!"

I turned and stared with wide eyes as my dad, Galahad Brimstone, hurried toward me. "You're here, too?" It was rare to find my parents in the same place for longer than five minutes.

His hug was warm and smelled of cloves as he embraced me. "Of course. We both got the news."

I stepped back, tears in my eyes as I gripped their hands. I was so stunned by their arrival that I didn't know what to say.

"We've been with Albert all morning," my dad said. "He's doing well and had a good night. The doctors are hopeful they can release him in a few days."

"That's great. I was with him last night after they brought him in. How are his hands?"

Pained expressions crossed my parents' faces.

My mom shook her head. "They'll take a while to heal. He'll be out of action in the kitchen for a couple of months. It's such a shame. He has a real talent. This will be hard on him."

I winced. "Have you been by Fandango's?"

They both nodded, sympathy in their eyes.

"There's not much left," my dad said.

I bit my lip. "I still can't believe it happened."

"Look on the bright side. Now you have options."

My head tilted. "What do you mean?"

Dad glanced at my mom, who gave a small nod. "We know you stay here to support your uncle, and we've always admired your dedication to the family."

"Sure. That's part of the reason. Uncle Albert would be alone if I didn't stay. But I also love living in Witch Haven. And I have friends here. I've also started dating someone. This is my home."

"Oh! Who are you dating?" My mom's groomed eyebrows rose. "Is it serious? Will I meet him while I'm here?"

I raised a hand, instantly regretting mentioning Cole. "Most likely."

"If it's serious, he'll understand your passion for baking," my dad said. "We travel all the time and still make things work."

Mom's forehead wrinkled, but she said nothing to contradict him.

"Cole's a great guy, but that's not the point. What I'm trying to say is, I don't just stay here for Uncle Albert."

"But now you're free," my dad said. "And I have an opening in my business. It's perhaps not as high up as you'd hope for, but I can't be seen to be too indulgent to my only daughter." His confident smile didn't match my own shocked expression.

"You... want me to work with you?"

"It's one option," my mom said swiftly. "And I've always said you'd be welcome to join me. We can travel the world together."

"Cloris, we discussed this. Luna is best suited being with me. My connections span the globe. She could go anywhere and work with anyone she chooses."

Mom's eyes narrowed. "Luna would have the same excellent opportunities if she were with me. I'm as established as you. And easier to work with."

"Hold-up! I'm not going with anyone."

Mom shot a death stare at my dad before smiling at me. "I want the best for you. It's wonderful how you spend so much time with Albert, but there's a whole world out there, and people will want the delicious desserts you make. You must be a part of that. It's your birthright."

Low level panic shifted inside me, making me overheat. There was no way I could work with either of my parents. They'd know the second I baked something that I'd been living a lie for years.

Dad squeezed my arm. "There's no hurry. I'm here for as long as you need me."

"As am I," my mom said smoothly, a bite to her tone.

"Think it over. I've already spoken to Albert about him retiring. He could come spend time with either of us. He might even enjoy the travel," my dad said. "And no more early starts. He'd appreciate that."

"He wouldn't. Uncle Albert doesn't even have a passport. He rarely leaves Witch Haven. Why would he, when he has everything he loves right here?"

"Does he, though? Perhaps he's only staying because he thinks that's what you want," my dad said. "Witch Haven is a quaint place, but there's so much more out there for both of you."

"We've said enough," my mom said. "All of this must be overwhelming."

"Yes, you have, and it is." I shook my head. "And Uncle Albert needs me. You said his injuries will take time to heal, so I'm not abandoning him to go baking cake in the sunshine."

"I said nothing about abandoning him. Perhaps Albert could bake and travel, too. I could find him something part-time to keep him occupied," my dad said.

"Maybe he doesn't want to retire from the bakery. Sure, he's getting older, but his baking magic is on top form. We have queues out the door at Fandango's every day wanting his treats. He won't give that up."

"Perhaps he should," my mom said. "You've indulged your uncle for long enough. Spread your wings and take on new challenges."

Dad nodded sagely. "You've been playing it safe by staying here."

"I like safe. And I like here." I felt like stamping my foot. "My focus is on making sure Uncle Albert gets better. And he can do whatever he likes with Fandango's. He can rebuild it from scratch or hire a catering van and travel around serving festivals. I don't care, so long as he's healthy and smiling again."

"We'll talk about it later. Everyone is stressed by this difficult situation." Dad raised his eyebrows at my mom. "Where are you staying? We couldn't find you when we arrived last night."

I huffed out a breath. "With Odessa. She has the farmhouse on the edge of the village."

"Oh, that's right. She took over the family business. It's been such a long time since I've seen her," my mom said. "We're in the local bed-and-breakfast."

I edged away, needing to get distance from my parents. I'd forgotten how intense they could be. "I should go see Uncle Albert."

"He's asleep. I was just in with him." Dad smiled at me. "We've been with him for an hour this morning, but the doctors are strict on how many visitors he can have. How about we stay here this morning, then we can meet for lunch and you can take the afternoon shift?"

"That's a wonderful idea. And I want to hear all about your new boyfriend," my mom said.

I glanced along the corridor. I really wanted to see Uncle Albert but wouldn't disturb him if he was tired. "Sure. I'll come back later."

After giving my parents brief hugs, I headed out of the hospital. Although I was glad to see them, they were already taking over my life, just like they always did. They saw me as a puzzle to solve because I didn't chase the big dream of opening a string of bakeries or take on complex, lucrative catering jobs. But I wasn't leaving Witch Haven. Fandango's might be gone, but we'd get it back, and life would return to normal.

I looked back at the hospital. My life had never been normal. I'd gotten amazing at hiding what was wrong with me. One day, I knew it would come out. Maybe that day was almost here.

When my lack of talent and magic was revealed, I had no clue what I'd do. My parents would want nothing to do with me, and Uncle Albert would be ashamed of me. He'd hinted he knew something wasn't right, but I'd never told him I was such a magical failure.

Pulling back my shoulders, I marched toward the bakery. I'd find a way out of this muddle. I always did.

I slowed as I neared the charred remains of Fandango's, and a lump lodged in my throat. There was barely anything left. There was no sign of the structure that had stood there, and tape covered the front to discourage people from stepping into the blackened remains and poking about.

My vision misted with tears. I'd spent so many years in this place, and it was all gone. I cared nothing about the possessions I'd lost. Clothes and books could be replaced. All the happy hours I'd spent with my friends eating cake and gossiping or having fun with Uncle Albert and Earl were here. There was nothing left. Rebuilding it wouldn't be the same.

"Excuse me, can you help me?"

I swept my hand across my eyes to dislodge the tears and turned to see a tall guy in his mid-thirties with sandy brown hair and a warm smile. "I'll try. What do you need?"

The guy scratched his head. "I'm looking for a place called Fandango's. Everyone I spoke to said it was the best place to get food, but I've been all along the street and I can't find any bakery with that name."

"Oh! Actually, you're standing right outside it." I gestured to the blackened mess. "This used to be Fandango's. I worked here. My uncle owns it." I choked on the last few words and had to take a second to compose myself.

The guy's jaw dropped. "No way! Bad luck." He glanced over his shoulder, and it was only then I noticed a familiar large off-road vehicle on the other side of the street. He gestured to the people inside. "Guys, get over here. We have a food crisis."

A woman with a dark ponytail got out with two other men, and they walked over. They were dressed similarly as if they were going on a trek, in combat pants and all-weather jackets.

"What's the problem?" the tallest guy said.

"This was the place we were looking for to get our meals for the trip."

They all oohed and ahhed at what was left of my home.

"The bakery burned down last night," I said. "Are you here for a vacation?"

"Kind of. Sorry, I should have made the introductions. I'm Torin Magnus." The guy who'd been looking for the bakery extended his hand, and I shook it. "This is Elsa, Alaric, and Reuben. We're here on a treasure hunt."

"A treasure hunt?" I nodded at the others. "What treasure are you looking for?"

Elsa grinned. "These idiots have been planning the trip for months. I discovered them in an online chat forum talking about uncovering the mystical gem of Witch Haven."

I laughed. "Oh! That's an urban legend. Sorry to disappoint, but the gem is only a myth to attract tourists."

"Then it worked on us," Torin said. "We're here to finally uncover the truth."

Alaric, a short guy with a neat dark beard, nodded. "I've researched the gem for years. We're close to finding its location."

I nodded and kept on smiling. "If you say so. I've been hearing about the gem ever since I was a kid. We get groups here every year looking for it, and no one's ever found anything. Not even a hint of where it might be."

Alaric and Reuben grinned at each other.

"We have an edge on the competition," Reuben said.

"But we need food," Torin said. "This place was recommended to us."

"Hey, Luna!"

I turned and raised a hand as Killian Burrows loped over. He had shoulder-length shaggy blond surfer style hair and was tall and rangy. He helped with the forest treks and outward bound pursuits during the tourist season. Killian was braver than me. There were things in the woods around Witch Haven that had a habit of eating magic users or spiriting them away, never to be seen again.

"Hi, Killian. I didn't know you were already running the treks. It's early."

He gestured at the group. "I got an offer I couldn't refuse. And this party is convinced they know where the mysterious gem of Witch Haven is."

"So I've been hearing. Good luck with your search," I said.

Killian did a double take as he stared at what was left of Fandango's. "Whoa! What happened here?"

I shook my head and sighed. "We had a fire last night. I guess you haven't heard."

"No, we were setting up camp in the woods last night. This is our first visit into the village. I was counting on you and Albert for some amazing food to feed my hungry treasure hunters."

"I've been dreaming about your desserts," Elsa said. "Killian told us all about how incredible the food is."

I glanced at what was left of the building and then at their eager faces. With Fandango's out of operation, money would be tight. I had a little savings, and Uncle Albert had some, but it wouldn't last long. And although Uncle Albert said the insurance would cover a rebuild, it wouldn't hurt to have extra put by just in case.

"What kind of thing are you looking for?" I said.

"Plain and simple food and lots of it." A hopeful glint entered Killian's eyes. "We need three meals a day and snacks. Breakfast, lunch, dinner, and whatever else you can provide. It's hungry work hunting around the woods."

"We'll be caving as well," Torin said.

"Don't give away our secrets," Alaric said.

"Don't worry about me. I won't spread rumors you're hunting for the gem." I looked back at Fandango's. "If you don't mind simple food, soups, stews, sandwiches, that sort of thing, I could manage that."

"You're a lifesaver." Killian nodded at the group. "You lot look around while I grab the paperwork from the vehicle and sort a deal with Luna." He winked at me as he led me to his mud-splattered truck.

"It's not going to be up to our usual standard," I said. "I'll have to improvise with the equipment I use."

"No worries. Honestly, this lot are so gullible. They're paying double my usual rate, and I didn't even have to haggle. They offered it. They've got more money than sense, and there's a generous budget for food."

"That's just what I need. As you can see, business won't be booming for a while."

Killian climbed into the truck and hunted through a mess of papers on the dashboard. "Then you're welcome to the job. It's gutting what happened to the bakery. I always stop by when I'm working in the area."

I peered into his truck. The front seat was a mess of mud and straw. "What have you been carrying around in here?"

He grinned. "I often transport orphaned animals to the sanctuary in Hollow Cove. They have that huge place out there that takes in abandoned and injured creatures. Some of them like to ride up front, and I enjoy the company."

"Was your last companion a goat?" I picked off a piece of straw. It had a pungent goaty smell.

"Nope. Way more interesting than that. A winged shimmering horse. Only a foal. I think its mom must have died. He was on his own when I found him."

My eyes widened. "They're rare. You found it in our woods?"

"Yep. All alone and sad. I'm taking care of him." Killian glanced at the group who were wandering along the row of stores. "This gig was last minute, so I didn't get a chance to clean up. I'll stick those guys in the back so they don't have to deal with this mess. Here's the paperwork." He handed me details of what they were paying.

I stifled a squeak. "You weren't kidding about the food budget."

Killian laughed. "That'll see you right for a while. If you could show up every morning with our supplies, I'd be eternally grateful. I need this job to go smoothly since they're paying so well."

I couldn't turn down the money he was offering, and I didn't want to. I could make simple things in Odessa's kitchen. And she was always baking muffins, so I could add her pumpkin spice treats to the mix. "It's a deal. I'm sure we can make this work. When do you need me to start?"

"First thing tomorrow. I'll get them food for today, but then it's over to you and your Brimstone magic."

I nodded. I'd just scored my very first freelance job. Let's hope my magic was up to the challenge.

Chapter 4

"Are you sure we've got enough for them?" Odessa heaved a stuffed cooler over one arm as we left her farmhouse the next morning.

I was carrying an equally heavy basket, laden with breakfast supplies and sandwiches for the treasure hunting party. "There's plenty here. We made enough for eight people. This is just what they need. Thanks again for letting me use your kitchen."

"So long as you share some of the food with me, I'm more than happy for you to make use of it." Odessa waved at a row of scarecrows lined up along the fence. Some of them waved back. "It's been a while since we had a gem hunting party in the village."

"I still can't believe people fall for that myth." Gray clouds hung low in the sky, threatening more rain, but it was holding off. I hoped it would stay that way until we got back from delivering the food.

Odessa placed the cooler in her ancient green truck, and I handed her the basket. "I remember my grandparents talking about it. It's an ancient myth. It goes back hundreds of years."

I slid into the passenger seat as she started the engine. "Which means it can't be real. Someone would have found the treasure by now."

Odessa maneuvered the truck over potholes and onto the main road, heading east toward the woods.

The wood stretched back for miles, and although there were some walking routes and picnic areas for visitors, most of it was left wild for the supernatural creatures to roam around in. I wouldn't want to be here at night. But in the daytime, it was usually safe.

"Did you hear about the camping party that disappeared?" Odessa said. "It was about ten years ago."

"That never happened."

"It did! They must have gotten too close to the truth."

"Or they got bored and went home."

"Or a Big Foot captured them and took them away." Odessa shuddered. "Or a woodland nymph. Who knows what's lurking among the treetops."

"Things with fangs, claws, and powerful magic, which is why we won't hang around for long. We'll deliver this and get out of here." I smiled as we sped to our destination. "Killian's been great. He's already paid me in advance for the whole job."

"That's handy. How long are they staying?"

"They paid for seven days. But they could stay longer if they don't find the gem."

"Which means they'll be here forever, according to you." She grinned at me. "Aren't they worried about the curse attached to the gem?"

"I guess not. Besides, a gem that doesn't exist can't have a curse attached to it. That's impossible."

Odessa pursed her lips. "It's a nasty curse. It came from the portentous potion being fed into the gem when it was first formed."

"No one makes portentous potions. They'd get locked away for creating anything so deadly."

"I'm only telling you what I heard. And people say the curse was attached to the gem for a good reason. The gem has immortality powers, the ability to resurrect, and the power to destroy."

I shook my head. "I've also heard it can command armies of vampires and werewolves. It's not true."

Odessa was quiet for a few seconds. "If I had that gem, you know what I'd use it for?"

"Commanding an army of werewolves to dig over your pumpkin patch?"

She shook her head. "I'd resurrect Brodie. Wouldn't it be great to have him back?"

My heart stuttered. Odessa never talked about her lost love. "Of course. It would be amazing if he was still here."

She stared straight ahead, her hands tight on the steering wheel. "I keep hoping I'll find a way."

"A way to move on?"

"No! A way to get him back. I've spent a lot of time thinking about it. It's possible. I've heard it can be done." She glanced my way before returning her attention to the road. "What if this gem could do that? Maybe I should join this hunting party."

I needed to tread carefully around this topic. The second I said anything Odessa didn't like, she'd slam the door shut. "I know you miss Brodie. He was a great guy."

"He was the best guy. He was the only one for me." Her sigh hit my heart. "I'm not getting any younger, and I thought by the time I was thirty I'd have started a family. Brodie would have been an amazing father to our children."

"You have your scarecrows. They're your family of sorts."

Odessa sniffed. "And I love them, each and every one, even the misbehaving ones. It brings me joy to bring them to life and hand them over to other families so they can protect their homes and land. But it's not the same. You know that. When my Brodie... When he went, he took a part of me with him. And I want him back, and I want that piece of me back. I need to feel whole again."

I reached over and gave her a one-armed hug. "You seem whole to me. And happy."

"I can be. Sometimes."

"You know you can talk to me and the others any time you're feeling glum. We all know how hard it was when you lost Brodie."

"He's not gone forever. I'll get him back, one day." She said the words so softly, I almost missed them.

"Or you could find someone else. You're funny, smart, and make the most amazing pumpkin muffins I've ever eaten. You also have a hugely successful business, and you're easy on the eye. You're a catch."

A sad sigh slid from Odessa's lips. "I don't want anyone else. Brodie's the only one I need."

"You could try a date or two, see how it feels. There are other guys out there. And you must get lonely."

"How can I be lonely when I have such amazing friends and so many scarecrows? And you're dating that delicious werewolf. I can live my romantic encounters indirectly through you and Cole." Odessa grinned at me, although it looked strained. "Come on, we have hungry mouths to feed." She steered the truck around the corner as we reached the parking lot of the woods.

The truck shuddered and coughed as we pulled in.

"Uh-oh! That sounds bad." I gripped the handle on the door.

Odessa grimaced. "My truck hates these woods. He gets scared. Keep going, sweetie. Slide into a spot, and I promise I'll take you to the car wash later and get you all shiny."

The truck rattled and died, rolling slowly into a vacant parking space.

Odessa patted the steering wheel. "Good boy. I knew you could do it."

"How are we getting back if the truck's too scared to move?"

"I'll get him towed. At least we got here before he died. I have no desire to lug heavy coolers for miles."

We hopped out and grabbed the food before taking one of the few paths into the woods. The weak daylight faded as dense overhanging firs dripped moisture onto our heads.

Odessa stopped by a fork in the path. "Which way?"

I pointed left, and we followed the directions Killian had given me. After twenty minutes of slow walking through the trees, we came to a clearing where five tents were set up. There was a firepit in the middle and several upturned logs that looked like they'd been used as seats.

"Hello! Breakfast is here," I said.

Elsa emerged from a tent. "Great. I'm starving. Thanks for bringing the food here. This place isn't easy to get to."

"It's all part of the service." I set down the basket. "You've got croissants, fruit, rolled sweet pancakes, pumpkin muffins, and sausage and mustard baps for breakfast."

"Did someone say breakfast?" Reuben emerged from his tent, looking rumpled around the edges as if he'd slept in his clothes.

I nodded and smiled at him. "It's all here. The cooler contains your lunch and dinner. Killian said you didn't need drinks."

Elsa had already snuck out a strawberry and almond butter croissant and was eating it. "We're fine for coffee and water. We picked those up on the way. This food is amazing. Thanks so much for making this work. We couldn't believe it when we turned up at the bakery to find it burned down. Had you worked there long?"

I nodded. "All my life. I used to live above it."

Odessa sighed. "I'm already missing your uncle's pastries."

"It's only been a couple of days!"

"A woman has needs."

Killian and Alaric wandered over and help themselves to breakfast, and I introduced Odessa to the treasure hunters.

Killian winked at me. "Awesome food, Luna. I knew you'd deliver what we needed."

I grinned at him. "You're welcome. What treasure hunting plans have you got today?"

"We're focusing on two spots. One site was recorded by a search party over a hundred years ago," Alaric said. "I found a journal entry they left behind. They were so sure they were close to finding the gem."

"You seem dedicated to this search," I said.

"Of course. Imagine what you could do with a gem like that."

I shared a smile with Odessa. "We were talking about that on our way over here."

"If it's only one gem, how will you share it?" Odessa said.

"That's all been agreed," Elsa said. "We have a contract, stating we each get a set amount of time with the gem. We get it for three months and then pass it to the next person."

"What would you use it for?" I said. "Do you even know what it does and how long the effects last?"

"Alaric is our fount of knowledge when it comes to the gem," Reuben said. "He knows everything about it."

Alaric's round cheeks flushed. "I've made a study of it. I research rare and mythical artefacts and catalog my findings for the Society of Mystical Collections."

"That sounds fun," I said. "You must come across all sorts of oddities."

He nodded. "Including this gem, which is believed to offer immortality, among other things."

"Yes! Eternal life," Elsa said. "Imagine what you could do if you had an infinite amount of time."

I wrinkled my nose. "Wouldn't that get boring? And what would happen when everyone you cared about was gone?"

"I'd find new people to care about. Of course, I'd miss my current family, but I'd have all the time in the world to learn new skills and go on adventures. And I'd keep finding new love. I always find relationships get stale after a few years, anyway."

"Does this immortality come with not ageing, too?" I said. "You must get a lot of wrinkles after you've been alive for a few thousand years."

She arched an eyebrow. "I'm not surprised you're skeptical. Most people are."

"What about the resurrection power?" Odessa said. "Have you found any reports about that?"

I didn't miss the hint of hope in her voice.

"It's possible the gem can restore life," Alaric said. "I've seen several recorded entries saying it has restorative powers. Although what condition those who are restored to life come back in, it wasn't clear."

"You'd probably resurrect a mindless ghoul who'd want to chew your still beating heart," Reuben said.

Everyone chuckled, other than me and Odessa.

"Where's Torin?" Reuben said. "He's always first on the scene whenever there's food around."

"He's still underground. He was poking around in that cave, setting up lighting so we can explore after breakfast," Elsa said. "I'll go—"

There was a muffled bang and a yelp. A few seconds later, smoke drifted toward us.

"That came from underground." Killian dropped his half-eaten muffin as he raced away.

We were all close on his heels.

"Torin! Are you down there, buddy?" Killian was on his knees by a smoking hole in the ground.

Odessa gripped my arm. I peered into the hole, hoping to see Torin emerge unharmed.

"I'm going in," Killian said.

"It's not safe down there," Elsa said. "What if there are more explosions?"

"Torin could be injured or trapped. We can't leave him." Killian grabbed the top of the ladder poking out of the hole and slid down it.

We all waited around the entrance in anxious silence.

"He's in here!" Killian's voice was muffled. "He's alive but hurt."

There was a groaning, and a few moments later, Torin's blackened face appeared.

Reuben and Alaric crowded around the hole to help him.

"Careful of my arm. It might be broken." Torin's eyebrows looked singed.

They eased him out of the hole, taking care not to touch the arm he had pressed against his chest.

Killian came out a few seconds later. "I need to get you to the hospital. That arm is a mess."

"What happened down there?" Elsa said.

"I don't know. I was hanging up lights, and this weird smell filled the cave. I was trying to find where it was, when there was a flash of light and

I was flung to the ground." Torin winced as he touched his arm. "I hit rock as I went down."

"We need to get a move on," Killian said. "The truck's not far. Are you okay to walk?"

Torin nodded. "I'll be okay."

"Can we come with you?" I said. "My uncle's in the hospital. I was heading there once I dropped off your food, but Odessa's truck broke down as we arrived, so we've no way back."

"Sure. Let's move, though. I don't like the look of that arm, and my healing magic won't touch it. It's not a skill of mine." Killian walked alongside Torin as we headed to the truck, helping him every time he stumbled.

The truck was parked a few minutes' walk from the clearing, and once Torin was settled in the back seat, we climbed in beside him.

I looked out the window of Killian's truck as he drove off. The anxious faces of Elsa, Reuben, and Alaric stared back at me.

Odessa leaned over the seat and gave a loud sniff. "It smells like a farmyard in here."

Killian chuckled. "Don't mind that. I still haven't had a chance to get this thing cleaned out. I scrubbed out the back seats as best I could, but that's as luxurious as it gets around here."

"Killian transports orphaned animals to the Hollow Cove sanctuary," I said.

Odessa's eyes widened, and she clasped her hands together. "How wonderful. I've been meaning to take a trip over there on one of their open days. I'll have to do a bake sale and raise them some money."

"They'd appreciate that. They need all the help they can get," Killian said. "How are you doing, Torin?"

"Hanging on in there," he said through gritted teeth. His face was pale as he sat rigidly in the seat.

Odessa nudged me. "Do you think it was the portentous potion?"

I shook my head at her. Now wasn't the best time to bring that up.

Torin frowned. "There's no dangerous potion or curse attached to the gem. That's been made up to keep people away and stop them from finding it."

"I'm not so sure," Odessa said. "Over the years, several groups who've tried to find it left early because they got scared. Isn't that right, Killian?"

He lifted a hand from the steering wheel. "Some of them aren't tough enough to handle the camping, but the curse has never gotten any of the people I've taken to the woods. I run a professional operation."

"You've not seen anything that makes you think the gem doesn't want to be found?" I said.

"Can't say I have. And nothing stops me from doing my job and making sure my clients have the best experience," Killian said.

"The explosion in the cave had nothing to do with a curse," Torin said. "It was just magic gone wrong. I must have misjudged a spell. It happens to the best of us."

Odessa didn't look convinced, but I nodded in agreement. I knew all about messing up magic.

We arrived at the hospital, and Killian helped Torin to get checked in.

"I'm just going to check on Uncle Albert," I said to Odessa. "I won't be long."

"I need to sort out getting my truck towed back to the farmhouse. Shall I meet you outside in ten minutes?"

I nodded then hurried to Uncle Albert's room. I slowed when I heard angry voices. That sounded like my mom and dad fighting. The door to the visitors' room was ajar, and I stopped beside it.

"She should come with me. She's my daughter." Mom sounded unusually shrill.

"She's also my daughter."

My eyebrows flashed up toward my hairline. I'd never heard my dad sound so tense.

"You know I have better connections. You simply need to say my name and doors open. It's just what she needs. Luna has been too sheltered here. She's not living up to her full potential," my dad said.

"She can do that by my side. I can take her to Paris, where she can re-sit some of the exams she didn't do so well in. Then Luna can pick a mentor from any number of incredible Parisian bakers. It's every woman's dream to spend the summer in Paris eating cake."

"Maybe she'd rather spend the summer in Antigua or Mexico or anywhere she likes. I can take her. I'll look after her."

I took a step back. They were still deciding my future and not bothering to ask me what I wanted. I couldn't handle them bickering over what to do with me, so I snuck off and peeked into Uncle Albert's room. He was fast asleep, so I decided not to disturb him.

Killian was waiting in the reception area when I hurried out.

"How's Torin doing?" I asked.

"They've got him in a cubicle. They'll take a look at him soon. I'll wait here and make sure he's okay. There won't be much else going on at the camp to worry about."

"Thanks for the lift to the hospital," I said.

"Anytime. How's your uncle doing?"

"He's sleeping. I'll come back and see him later. I'll see you at the camp tomorrow with fresh supplies?"

"Sure thing."

I headed outside and discovered Odessa studying a spiky bush with intense interest. She was chewing on what looked like a piece of dried pumpkin.

She turned as I approached and smiled at me. "That was quick. I was just thinking about grabbing a coffee while you saw your uncle."

"Another time. He's asleep. And we need to get out of here."

"Why? Are we being chased?" Odessa trotted along beside me.

"Worse. My parents are making plans for me. And they don't involve staying here."

"Oh! That's bad." She glanced over her shoulder. "Shouldn't you talk to them about that?"

"Another time." Which wouldn't be soon. I had enough complications in my life without domineering parents.

"Are you sure your truck is up to this trip?" We were headed back to the camp the next morning with fresh supplies for the treasure hunters.

"He'll make it. I cast a protection spell over him so he feels safer going into the woods." Odessa reached a hand into the bag of candied pumpkin that sat between us.

"You're almost as bad as Earl and his catnip."

"What do you mean?"

"The candied pumpkin. It seems addictive."

"It's fine. It's pumpkin. It's a health food."

"What about the sugar sprinkles all over it?"

"They're for decoration." Odessa popped another one in her mouth. "Help yourself."

I shook my head. "I'm good. But I wish you could cast a protection spell on me, so I'm protected against my parents whisking me away." I'd filled her in on all the plans being made for me.

"But your mom wants to whisk you to Paris." Odessa sighed. "The city of love. And all those amazing pastries. It doesn't sound bad."

"It's about a million miles from here. They can keep Paris and its pastries."

"You should speak to them about it. And they were only fighting because they want what's best for you."

"They think they know what's best for me. But they're so focused on getting me some stressful job in a high-class bakery, they haven't bothered to ask me if that's what I want."

"Isn't it? Aren't all Brimstones destined for greatness when it comes to desserts?"

I jutted out my bottom lip. "That's the theory, but I don't know. And Earl said something the other day that's been playing on my mind."

"Does it involve catnip?"

I smiled. "For once, no. But he's not happy, and he blames me."

"I've barely seen him since you moved into the farmhouse. He's not usually this elusive."

"That's also my fault. We're not talking at the moment."

Odessa hummed under her breath for a few seconds. "You don't really treat Earl like a familiar. It's not the same as how Indigo is with hers. They're always involved when she's spell casting and needs a magic boost. You have a different bond with Earl."

"He said the same thing. I'm not sure I have much of a bond with him at all. He even suggested he finds a new witch."

"He can't mean that. I'm sure Earl is happy with you. You're just going through a rough patch."

"Nope. I imagine he's already buffing his resume and putting the paw out to see if anyone is in the market for a black cat familiar."

"Perhaps you could try including him more. He might feel left out."

"I would, but he never helps. A witch's familiar is supposed to enhance her magic, but when Earl adds to my baking spells, they turn into disasters. He blows up more cakes than me. And he hasn't helped with a spell for ages." I sighed and looked out the window. "Maybe I should do more with Earl, though. I have to find something he enjoys doing."

"You could try different spells. How is he with healing magic?"

"No idea. He doesn't get involved in any magic I use."

"Is that because he doesn't want to or because you exclude him?"

"A bit of both." I had a problem when it came to Earl, but I also had a tricky balancing act to manage. Earl didn't know about my magic harem containing Ridley, Gloria, and Faye or the farmhouse I kept them hidden in.

I'd gotten so used to keeping secrets from him that it had become second nature. He must have picked up on that. And a witch should never keep secrets from her familiar.

Odessa pulled the truck into the parking lot without incident, although the engine grumbled several times. We unpacked the food and made our way into the camp.

Elsa was the first to join us. She yawned and nodded her thanks as Odessa handed over a filled cheese and ham rolled pancake.

Reuben stumbled out of his tent a few minutes later. He scrubbed his forehead and groaned. "I shouldn't have had that last beer. My head is throbbing."

"I'm not feeling too great either." Elsa glanced at me. "Since Torin didn't come back from the hospital last night, we drank his beer and our own. We stayed up late talking around the fire. I'm regretting that now, though."

"Any word about Torin?" I said.

"He'll be fine," Reuben said. "We dropped by to see him yesterday afternoon. They kept him overnight to keep an eye on things, but he should be back any time now."

"Where's Alaric?" I said. "Will he have a sore head, too?"

"I shouldn't think so," Reuben said. "He sometimes gets up early and goes for a walk before we start. Maybe he's already out. He'd better hurry, or I'll eat his breakfast. And we need him to light the fire. He's a pro with fire magic. We never have to worry about the flames going out when he's around."

"I'll go get him. His tent is the one at the end, isn't it?"

Elsa nodded. "That's right. But tell him not to hurry if he's having a lie-in. It'll be a slow start for all of us this morning, and Reuben will have to light the campfire the old-fashioned way." She shook a box of matches at him.

I headed to Alaric's tent and slapped my hand against it several times. "Alaric, it's Luna. Breakfast is here."

He didn't reply.

"Are you in there?" I undid the zipper on the tent and poked my head inside. A strong metallic smell filled my nose, and I staggered back as I took in the horrific sight in front of me.

Alaric was on the floor in a pool of blood.

Chapter 5

"Luna, what's wrong?" Odessa hurried over as I gave a strangled cry of alarm, my hand covering my mouth.

I pointed at the tent, unable to get enough air in my lungs to speak.

She peeked inside and gasped before backing away and stumbling into me. "Is he…"

I nodded. "I think so. We should check, though. But there's so much blood."

"What's going on over there?" Reuben said. "Tell that lazy nerd to hurry."

I swallowed and finally grabbed in some air. "Alaric won't be joining you for breakfast. You both need to see this."

Reuben and Elsa must have heard the horror in my voice because they dashed over.

Elsa dropped her croissant and turned away the second she saw Alaric's body.

"He's been stabbed!" Reuben said.

I mustered up some courage and peered back into the tent. I'd missed it at first, because Alaric was on his side with his hands by his stomach, but there was a knife lodged in his gut.

My insides clenched as I took a step closer. "That knife belongs to me. I brought it yesterday with your food. I didn't mean to leave it behind."

"Hey, what's everyone up to over there?"

I turned at the sound of Torin's voice. "There's been... an incident."

"What kind of incident?" Torin's arm was in a sling. "I knew everyone would slack off because I wasn't around."

"Torin, something awful has happened," Elsa said. "It's Alaric. He's dead."

"What?" Torin froze for a second then hurried over. "Are you joking with me?"

"It's no joke." Reuben's expression was grim.

We all stared inside the tent.

"We should get the Magic Council involved," Odessa whispered to me.

I frowned, but she was right. This couldn't have been an accident. I turned to face the group, partially blocking their view of Alaric's body. "We shouldn't touch anything. There could be evidence in there."

Elsa startled, and her gaze shot to me. "Evidence? You think this was murder?"

"He hardly stumbled and fell on the knife," Reuben muttered.

"I just... I don't understand." Elsa shook her head. "Did you say that knife was yours, Luna?"

"Yes. I recognize the design on the handle. It's the one I usually carry in my purse."

"Why do you carry a knife in your purse?" Torin said.

"You never know when there'll be a slicing emergency. It's meant to cut cake, not..." I gestured behind me.

"What was Alaric doing with your knife?" Reuben said.

"I must have left it behind with the food. I don't know why he had it in his tent," I said. "Odessa, could you get someone from the Magic Council? The sooner they see this, the better."

She nodded. "Of course. I won't be long."

I gently ushered the group away from Alaric's tent and lowered the zipper to give him some dignity. Everyone gathered around the cold firepit, all seeming too shocked to speak for several minutes.

"Who would do this to Alaric?" Torin finally said. "He was a decent guy. I can't imagine anyone wanting to hurt him."

Elsa swiped at her eyes. "You're right. He was nice, quiet. This makes no sense. Are you sure this couldn't have been an accident? Alaric was really clumsy. He was always tripping over things. Maybe he tripped and..."

Reuben slumped onto an upturned tree stump. "He was the brains of our operation, but he was a klutz. He was the one who gathered most of the research that brought us here. Alaric loved his books and maps."

I nodded. Maps had been scattered all around his tent. "It sounds like he took the hunt for the gem seriously."

"It was his obsession." Elsa's voice was shaky. "He never married and has no kids, so he spent his free time researching obscure references about hidden magical treasures. When I first got on board with this, I thought he was joking, but he's been researching this site for years."

"You don't think that's the reason he was stabbed, do you?" Torin said.

"Someone killed him because they didn't want him to have the gem?" Reuben's gaze darted around the trees. "Do you think that someone is watching us to see if we'll continue the treasure hunt?"

I tensed and looked around. No one said anything, but we were all scanning the trees.

A truck door slammed, and a moment later, Killian arrived. "Hey, everyone. Ready for a day of treasure hunting?" His smile faded as he looked around the group. "Has something happened?"

Reuben pointed at Alaric's tent. "Alaric is dead."

Killian staggered back as if someone had punched him. He looked at me as if for confirmation.

I nodded. "I found him. He's been stabbed."

Killian strode to Alaric's tent and looked inside before anyone stopped him.

I hurried over and caught hold of his arm. "Maybe you shouldn't poke around."

The color was gone from his face as he turned to me. "Who did this?"

"We're not sure. Someone from the Magic Council is on their way. They'll investigate and find out what happened to him."

Killian rubbed a hand down his face. "This couldn't have been an accident?"

"I don't see how. If Alaric fell on that knife, he's the unluckiest guy I know. Do you know much about him?"

He scrubbed at the back of his neck. "Not really. Alaric kept to himself. I asked if he was okay a few times, but he seemed happy enough. He said he liked the quiet. He was pretty introverted, but that was cool. I just don't get this."

There was a shift in the air pressure, and a second later, a spell materialized Devlin Goody and a colleague in the middle of the clearing.

He stared at me, rolled his eyes, and then shook his head. "What trouble have you got yourself into this time, Luna?"

I tipped back my head and sighed just as it started to rain. Why did it have to be my archenemy from the Magic Council sent to solve this murder?

Devlin marched over to me. "Odessa said there'd been an incident. Someone is dead."

"Alaric Raven," Elsa said. "He's in his tent."

"And why are you here?" Devlin glared at me.

I needed to tackle this head-on before he jumped to the wrong conclusion. "Alaric's part of a treasure hunting group looking for the mysterious gem of Witch Haven."

Surprise showed in Devlin's eyes before he nodded. "Go on."

"I'm here to provide the catering. I delivered the food this morning with Odessa, but Alaric didn't come out of his tent. I went over to wake him and discovered him inside. It looks like he's been stabbed. And I'll come clean about the murder weapon. The knife sticking in him belongs to me. It'll have my fingerprints on it, and possibly Odessa's, but neither of us had any reason to kill Alaric."

Devlin took a few seconds to take in this information. He looked at his colleague. "Seal that tent. Make sure no one goes in."

His colleague nodded and positioned himself in front of the tent.

I blinked in surprise. That was easier than I'd thought it would be. Usually, when Devlin finds me at a crime scene, he tries to arrest me.

"Who's in charge here?" he said.

"I guess that would be me." Torin raised his hand.

"And you are?" Devlin walked over to him, his notebook out.

I swiftly followed, keen to learn more about this treasure hunting group.

"Torin Magnus." He pointed at Elsa. "This is Elsa Cane and Reuben Deadwood. You probably know Killian."

Devlin scribbled down the details before looking at Killian and nodding. "And your reasons for being here?"

"Just as Luna told you. We're looking for the mysterious gem of Witch Haven," Torin said.

Devlin took down the information. "Alaric was doing that, too?"

Elsa nodded. "He got together most of the resources we needed to pinpoint the areas to look in."

The rain intensified, and everyone moved out of the clearing and under the shelter of some thick fir trees.

Devlin looked at his colleague. "Start processing the scene. We don't want anything to get washed away."

His colleague cast a spell over the clearing. It shimmered from side to side as it hunted for evidence.

Devlin turned back to the group. "Talk me through what happened. When was the last time anyone saw Alaric alive?"

"I've only just got back from the hospital." Torin pointed at his sling. "I got injured on site yesterday morning. The doctor kept me for observation overnight. The last time I saw Alaric was yesterday morning around eight-thirty."

"How did you hurt your arm?"

"There was an explosion in one of the caves we're planning to investigate."

"You're using explosive materials here? Do you have a permit?"

"No! Not dynamite, nothing like that. My magic must have misfired." Torin shrugged one shoulder. "It was my fault, and I was the only one injured."

"I saw Alaric about ten-thirty last night," Elsa said. "I was sitting by the firepit with Reuben, and we were chatting and having a few drinks. Alaric stayed for one, but he's not a big drinker and said he had research to do. He left us and went into his tent. That was the last time I remember seeing him."

Reuben nodded. "That sounds about right. His light stayed on for about an hour. It went off before midnight. I figured he'd gone to sleep. He's an early riser."

"Did either of you hear Alaric get up in the night? Or hear any confrontation or fight he had with his attacker?" Devlin said.

They both shook their heads.

"No, nothing like that," Reuben said. "But we'd had a lot to drink last night. And I always sleep like the dead after a few beers. I didn't hear anything from Alaric's tent."

"Same here," Elsa said. "I turned in about midnight."

Devlin looked at Killian. "What about you?"

"I left the camp yesterday evening about seven o'clock. I made sure the campers had everything they needed for the night and then went back to my place. I've got a room on the edge of the village near the old Macintyre farm. It's a ten-minute drive from here. The last time I saw Alaric, he was sitting by the firepit with Elsa and Reuben having dinner. I only learned what happened to him when I arrived this morning."

"None of you saw or heard anything suspicious?" Devlin said.

"I didn't hear anything odd coming from Alaric's tent," Elsa said, "but there was a weird noise in the night. It freaked me out. I even looked out the tent to see what it was."

"What kind of noise?" I said.

Devlin glared at me. "Could you describe the noise?"

"I'm embarrassed to say, but it sounded like a ghostly groan. I heard it several times. It gave me the chills. It was a sort of honk-bark-groan."

Devlin's eyebrows rose. "A ghostly groan? Could it have been a wild animal? We have supernatural creatures in the woods. Perhaps one of them came around the tents and scared you."

"It's possible. In the end, I figured it was just the wind making weird noises through the trees. Although I saw an animal when I looked out, it was small. I doubt it was that making so much noise."

"What kind of animal?" Devlin said. "Some of the woodland creatures can sound eerie."

"This one was cute. And he had a mark on his leg. I think it was blue, but I couldn't tell for sure because it was dark. I thought I might have imagined it. I really need to give up drinking."

"And what time was this?"

"The early hours of the morning. Maybe two or three?"

The rain grew faster, slamming down so hard it was getting through the thick branches of the trees.

"If this weather gets much worse, we won't be able to do any treasure hunting today," Killian said.

"I suggest you don't." Devlin looked at the increasingly muddy clearing and frowned. "And any evidence will be washed away if we don't hurry."

"Why doesn't everyone come back to my farmhouse?" Odessa said. "It's not far, and it's warm and dry. And I'm sure none of you want to stay here with everything that's going on. You can camp in the fields if you'd like or use a barn. Although you'll need to watch out for the scarecrows."

"That sounds like a good plan. I'm not keen on staying here." Torin's gaze went to Alaric's tent.

"I can take you all in the truck," Killian said.

"Very well," Devlin said. "Stay close by, though, and no one is to leave the village. I'll have more questions for you once we've taken a look around the crime scene."

I was torn between staying and going with the others, but a sharp look from Devlin had me scurrying away. I could tell when I wasn't wanted.

Once everyone was inside Killian's truck, they followed me and Odessa back to her farmhouse.

"I can't believe what's going on," she said. "I didn't have much to do with Alaric, but he seemed nice enough, and he was always polite. Who'd want him dead?"

"It's got to be someone on the treasure hunt. Alaric wasn't local, so no one around here had a grudge against him."

"You think it was Torin, Elsa, or Reuben?"

"I can't think of anyone else it would be. Although Reuben made me nervous when he suggested someone snuck out of the woods and killed Alaric because of the gem. But I doubt anyone's lurking around, waiting for a chance to strike. And why kill Alaric and not the others? They're all after the same thing."

"That means we've been serving food to a killer."

"Maybe so, but why would any of them want Alaric dead? As you said, he was a nice guy. He kept to himself and didn't seem to cause trouble in the group."

"Storm always says you need to watch out for the quiet ones. Maybe there was something dark going on we don't know about."

"Elsa said Alaric was the brains behind the operation, so why get rid of the cleverest person in the group? It puts them at a disadvantage."

"You don't think... No, he couldn't have managed it, could he?" Odessa shook her head as she grabbed a handful of candied pumpkin from the bag between the seats.

"Go on. What were you going to say?"

She glanced at me. "What if Alaric found the gem? He discovered it and tried to keep it a secret. One of the others found out. There was a fight, and Alaric was killed."

I shuddered. "If that's true, someone in the group has a powerful magical weapon, and they've just killed to get their hands on it."

"If someone took the gem from Alaric, why stick around?"

"To avoid becoming the prime suspect in a murder investigation."

"They wouldn't care about that. They'd basically be impossible to kill if they evoked its immortality power."

"You can still be immortal and get arrested for murder. Maybe they're keeping quiet and hoping someone else will get the blame. Or they're throwing us off the scent by suggesting a secret lurker snuck into the camp and committed the crime."

"Reuben suggested that. Do you think it was him?"

"It could be any of them."

"And what about the ghostly groan Elsa heard? Could that be connected?"

"That could have been the wind or one of the hundreds of spooky creatures in the woods." I glanced over my shoulder at the receding trees. "You'd never catch me camping in that place."

"Or it could have been the gem curse," Odessa said. "Alaric was getting too close to the truth, so the curse activated and took him out."

"How could a curse stab a person? I sort of understand a magical explosion, but Alaric was stabbed. And with my knife. Why do that when you could give him a gross illness or plague without having to get all stabby and covered in blood?"

"Whatever's going on, I don't like being involved. I shouldn't have invited them to the farmhouse, but I can't un-invite them. That would look rude."

"You've done an excellent thing. Now, we've got all the suspects under one roof." I leaned over and snagged a piece of candied pumpkin from the bag. "And look on the bright side, at least Devlin doesn't think I did it."

"Give him time. He'll find a reason to implicate you."

I swiped her arm. "You're not even the tiniest bit funny."

Odessa switched her wipers to double fast action as the rain beat down. "This weather doesn't seem natural to me. We were forecast sunshine all day. What if it's also the curse? It's wiping away evidence of Alaric's murder so no one can prove it did it."

"You're talking about the curse like it's a living thing. We don't even know if it's anything more than a myth." I leaned back in my seat. "But something awful happened at that campsite, and we were in the middle of it. We need to play it cool when we get to yours. If the killer is in that group, we don't want to scare them away."

"I won't say a word about our murder theories. If one of them has that gem, I don't want them using it on me."

We pulled up outside her farmhouse and climbed out of the truck. Killian was right behind us, and within a couple of minutes, everyone was inside and settled around Odessa's kitchen table.

She bustled about, making coffee for everyone and serving pumpkin pancakes, even though no one said they wanted anything to eat.

I gestured for her to stop flapping and take a seat. She gave a pointed stare at the group before finally settling in a chair.

"We should have paid attention to what happened the first morning we were here." Reuben huffed out a laugh.

"What happened? Did someone tell you to leave the area?" I said.

He shook his head. "I was sort of joking, but I meant the gem curse. Maybe we unleashed something we shouldn't. Torin getting hurt was a sign of the trouble to come."

"We don't believe in the curse," Torin said. "You know that explosion was my mistake."

"You said there was a strange smell just before it happened," Elsa said. "What if that was the curse telling you to stop poking around before it's too late?"

No one spoke for several long, awkward minutes as we mulled over this unsettling possibility. I didn't believe in the gem or the curse, but these arguments had me wondering.

Odessa kept nodding at me and looking around the group.

"Don't worry about the curse," I said. "And the gem isn't real. I've lived here most of my life, and it's a joke among the locals. We play up the curse and the hidden gem because visitors love it. Sorry to say, it simply isn't true. It's only a tourist lure."

"Alaric thought otherwise and look what happened to him," Reuben said.

Torin nodded. "And the landowner agreed with us about the gem being real. He knows it's out there somewhere. He gave us his approval to look for it."

"You had to get permission to hunt for the gem?" I said.

Killian nodded. "I always check with Bart Hogarth out of courtesy, so he knows there'll be people out there. He's usually fine about it, but it is his land."

"And we made an informal deal," Torin said. "If we found the gem, he'd get fifty percent of the profits."

"Profits? You planned to sell it?" Odessa said.

"No! We'd share it." Reuben shrugged and looked a little sheepish. "Although we only agreed to that to keep the old guy happy. After all, we were doing the hard work. I'd have given him some money to keep him sweet, but he wasn't getting his hands on that gem."

I sat back as they continued to talk about whether to keep treasure hunting. The idea of getting fifty percent of a rare, powerful gem was an excellent motive for murder. Or maybe Bart had had enough of treasure hunters on his land and decided to set an example to discourage more people from traipsing around his woodland.

After spending half an hour with the group, I made my excuses to leave.

Odessa followed me out and eased the front door shut behind her. "You've got that look in your eyes. What are you going to do?"

I grinned. She knew me too well. "First, I'm going to see Uncle Albert and spend time with him, then I'm having a word with Bart. Maybe he knows what happened last night."

"You're leaving me alone with a bunch of killers?"

"One killer. And we haven't figured out which one of them did it."

"Still, I don't feel safe in my home. You can't leave me." Odessa clutched my arm.

"Round up some of your meanest scarecrows. They'll keep your guests company. And Earl is around here somewhere. He'll keep an eye on things."

"Oh! I suppose so. But if any of them make a wrong move, the scarecrows will attack." She stuck her fingers in her mouth and whistled.

A few seconds later, six huge scarecrows with glowing eyes and grimaces on their faces were lined up in front of her.

"Be discreet," I whispered. "If the killer realizes we're on to them, they could do something dangerous."

"My boys are always discreet."

I arched an eyebrow.

Odessa shrugged. "Fine. They're mostly discreet. Boys, you're to guard the farmhouse and watch my guests. Don't make it obvious, but we have a lethal killer on our hands. They might have the power of immortality, so it'll be a brutal fight when it goes down."

The scarecrows advanced toward the farmhouse in a giant, menacing mass, the ground shaking beneath their feet.

"Whoa! Hold fire on the talk of showdowns. Keep your guests happy and fed. If anyone starts acting odd, bring in the scarecrows. With any luck, our killer will want a quiet exit from this situation, the same as us, so no brutal fighting will be needed."

Odessa raised a hand, and the scarecrows stopped. "Boys! No bloodbath unless called for."

I blew out a breath. "That'll do. I'll be back this evening. Let me know if you have any problems."

She grinned at me. "We'll crack this case wide open."

I hurried away. I didn't care about cracking it open as much as getting out the other side alive.

Chapter 6

"I'm certain staying here isn't the best thing for you." Mom sat in a chair in Uncle Albert's hospital room.

My dad was in a chair on the opposite side of the bed. "Your mother has a point. After everything you've told us about this murder, Witch Haven doesn't seem like a safe place to live. It's gone downhill since my last visit."

I'd spent the morning with Uncle Albert and my parents, and my patience was running out. I was always happy to spend as much time as I could with my uncle, but I'd forgotten how intense my parents were. They constantly asked questions and grilled me about the bakery and what new recipes I was working on. And after I'd told them about Alaric's murder, the intense questioning only got worse.

"There's nothing to worry about. It's being looked into by the Magic Council. And it's not like people get killed all the time in Witch Haven. It's a safe place," I said.

"It's not all that safe," my dad said.

"Sure, we get the occasional magical mishap, but I enjoy living here. And you always let me play outside when I was a kid. You wouldn't have done that if you didn't think it was safe."

"Places change. And it seems Witch Haven has altered over the years." My dad leaned forward in his seat. "I've also heard about your problems."

I glanced at Uncle Albert, who seemed to be struggling to stay awake. "My problems?"

"Just because I'm busy working away, it doesn't mean I don't keep up-to-date with the family news."

I gulped. Did he mean my magic failing? He'd found out what I'd been hiding? "Those are rumors. Pay no attention to them."

"Rumors? I'm talking about the time you were abducted. It didn't happen?" my dad said.

"Oh! That was sorted out ages ago. And I don't think I was ever in real danger."

"I was gravely concerned not to know about this until after the event."

"So was I." Mom glared at him.

"What would either of you have done? Come into limbo and rescued me?"

Dad sat straight in his seat. "If that was needed. I'd have made sure you were in no harm."

"I was safe. My friends looked out for me. You know I have amazing friends."

"From what I heard, it was one of those friend's mothers who took you," my mom said. "And Indigo Ash isn't what I call a suitable friend. I've always had concerns about her."

"No, you haven't. And you can stop right there. Indigo is my best friend, and she never gave up on me. She's one of the many things that makes this place so special." I caught hold of Uncle Albert's hand.

He smiled at me. "I always look out for Luna. And she's right, her friends are always there for her. They're spirited witches with plenty of power."

"I also know that wasn't the only incident of dark magic in Witch Haven," my dad said. "You yourself were influenced, Albert. You both kept quiet about that. I had to hear the terrible news from other people."

"What other people?" I said.

"I have my resources. And I need to use them, since you two are keeping secrets from me."

"From us." Mom's glare intensified. "We both need to be kept informed of any struggles you might have."

Resources? Was my dad spying on us? I glanced at Uncle Albert, but he seemed as confused as I was about the situation. "We said nothing because we know how busy you both are. It would break your hearts to give up your work for something so small."

"My only daughter going missing isn't considered a small matter," my mom said. "I worry about you."

"You don't have to. I can look after myself. And if ever I have trouble, Uncle Albert is here. He's great at helping me if ever I need it. He always has been."

He squeezed my hand. "And I don't mind a bit. But I'm not getting any younger. I don't want you to stay here just because of me."

My gaze narrowed as I turned it on my parents. "Have they been pressuring you to say that?"

Uncle Albert looked away. "Perhaps it's for the best if you try living somewhere else. There's a big world out there, and Witch Haven is only a tiny part of it."

"Especially if the village is no longer a suitable place to live. And you'd be welcome to come with me when I leave. I can find you a place to live, a new job, and you'll have everything you need," my dad said.

"No, I won't. I won't have my home here or my friends and family around me."

"We're your family," my dad said.

"You know what I mean." I tilted my head at Uncle Albert.

Dad folded his arms across his chest. "I'm also aware you became entangled in a murder. You were a prime suspect in the poisoning of Jinti Calrook. Why didn't you tell me about that?"

I massaged my forehead with my fingers. "Because I was innocent, and the Magic Council had it all wrong. Why stress you out when there's no need?"

"And you've been tangling with the Magic Council ever since that unfortunate incident," my mom said.

"Do you have a spy camera hidden in the bakery? How do you know all this?"

Dad simply shrugged. "When the family reputation is at stake, it's important to squash rumors before they get ugly."

I didn't know how to respond. That wasn't a denial about any potential hidden camera or magic spyware tracking me.

"And is it true, someone from the Magic Council investigated Fandango's?" my mom said. "They had concerns about the magic used?"

Uncle Albert lifted a hand. "You're making it sound like Luna's been doing terrible things. When she was taken, she had no control over the unstable dark magic user. And she solved Jinti's murder, found the killer, and cleared her name. Your daughter is a genius."

"Jinti's murder was actually a suicide. But I solved an old murder and confronted the killer." I lifted a hand as my mom's face paled. "But it's basically the same thing. It was all tied up together. And I was in barely any danger."

"Of course Luna's a genius," my dad said. "She's a Brimstone. That's not the topic of debate. My point is—"

"Our point," my mom said.

Dad blew out a breath. "Of course. Our point is you could do so much more. You'd never have become part of some dark magic conspiracy or embroiled in a tawdry murder if you were with me. You could travel the world making desserts for royalty and celebrities. You could have your pick of work and live in luxury. It's a fabulous life."

"My life is already fabulous," I said. "And I don't want all those fancy things. I have everything I need right here."

"You lived in a two-bedroom apartment above the bakery. Why limit yourself?" Dad's tone was sharp and condescending.

I glanced at Uncle Albert. I wasn't limiting myself. Every time I used my baking magic, it stretched me to breaking point.

My parents were on the wrong track with this argument. They were concerned with me not fulfilling my baking potential, not the fact I had no potential to fulfill. And how could I reveal that to them, when their reputation meant everything?

"If going with your father isn't of interest to you, you're welcome to join me," my mom said. "I already have three new commissions I'm considering. You can take one or act as my apprentice. Not that you need it, but there were classes you didn't excel in, so perhaps some skills need finessing."

"Your mother isn't being kind to you. Your baking is excellent. I would never make you take a refresher course. A Brimstone instinctually knows how to create excellence."

Mom's hands clenched in her lap. "I never said her baking wasn't excellent."

I waved a hand in the air to get their attention. "Thanks for the offers, but you both need to back off."

"You could pick the job we take on next," my mom persisted. "They're all excellent pay. You pick, and then I'll oversee things. And I won't interfere unless you want my assistance."

"Perhaps she doesn't want to go with you," my dad said.

"She does! Luna, we barely ever spend any girl time together."

"Stop! I'm not going with either of you." I shot desperate looks at them. "I appreciate the offers, but I don't want that lifestyle."

"We can discuss it another time," my mom said on a sigh. "You've been through a lot, finding that man stabbed to death. And, of course, we need to make sure Albert's capable of looking after himself when he gets out of the hospital."

"It's not about that! He's very capable without me, but I love living with Uncle Albert. And I love Witch Haven."

"Of course you do. We'll finalize matters later." Mom smoothed her skirt over her knees.

I recognized the determined look on her face. She wasn't letting this drop. I glanced at my dad and saw the same steely expression. They both wanted me to work for them and not stay here, and they weren't prepared to listen to a word I had to say on the matter.

The door opened, and a plump, round-faced nurse walked in with a tray. She had a warm smile and a twinkle in her blue eyes as her gaze settled on Albert. "How is my favorite patient doing?"

"I wouldn't mind some peace," he muttered.

"Sorry, Uncle Albert. We'll leave you alone. You need your rest." I went to move away from the bed, but he kept hold of my hand.

"You're not the problem," he whispered.

"We can't have you getting overexcited," the nurse said.

"You're too good to me, Tabitha."

I studied Uncle Albert, surprised by the change in his tone when he spoke to the nurse. And he appeared perkier as he sat up straight in his bed.

Tabitha giggled. "You're a dream patient. You never object when I ask to take your temperature, cast a healing spell, or give you your medicine. And you're responding so well to treatment. You might even get to go home a day early if you keep being such a good boy."

His cheeks flushed bright pink. "I promise to behave myself around you."

I grinned at Uncle Albert. Was he flirting with this nurse?

"You take your pills, then I need to ask your visitors to leave. You need a good couple of hours rest and some more healing magic." Tabitha flexed her fingers, and light blue sparkles glittered off them.

Uncle Albert obligingly took his pills and was happy to let Tabitha fuss around him, straightening his sheets and plumping his pillows.

"Two more minutes." She patted his shoulder before nodding at us and leaving the room.

"Do you have a crush on that nurse?" I leaned close to Uncle Albert. "She's pretty."

His cheeks grew even pinker. "She's excellent at her job. Some of the nurses can be sharp because they're so busy, but Tabitha is very sweet. She always makes time for me."

I dropped my jaw in mock surprise. "You like her!"

He didn't meet my gaze. "She's a pleasant woman."

It was such a temptation to tease him mercilessly, but I was thrilled for Uncle Albert. He'd been on his own for a long time, and it was long overdue he get back in the dating game. I didn't want him lonely, especially since my parents were pressuring me to move away. Not that I had any intention of going.

"We'll leave you to it, Albert." Mom kissed his cheek. "We'll get lunch and see you this afternoon."

"I'll see you all later."

"Albert." My dad nodded at him. He left the room with my mom close behind him.

"I'm not sure I'll be by anymore today," I said. "I promised Odessa I'd get back to her farmhouse before it got late. She's got the treasure hunters staying there."

"You're not poking around in this murder, are you? Your parents are already worried about you."

"Not really. Just a bit. I feel bad for the guy who was stabbed."

"Luna, you always get in trouble when you're involved in these mysteries. Didn't you hear what your parents said? If you get muddled up in this, they'll force you to leave Witch Haven."

"I'm not going anywhere. And don't listen to them about me not living a full life. I want to live with you. I've always lived with you." I glanced over my shoulder to make sure the door was closed. "I think of you more as a parent than either of them."

"Don't say that." A smile crossed his face. "Although it's sweet of you. They're your real parents."

"Sure, but you were always around for me when they were travelling and working. Sometimes, they seem like strangers. And they want such different things from life. It's not me. I don't fit their mold of the perfect baking princess."

He patted the back of my hand. "I'm glad you think of me so kindly. But I don't want to hold you back. Give some thought to what they said. With Fandango's gone, there'll be nothing for you to do here for months. I have no idea how long it'll take to rebuild, but we won't be up and running anytime soon."

"We might be. What about if we rented another building? Or got a pancake truck and drove it around? We could be serving food by the end of the month if that's what you want."

"Creating desserts and delicious treats will always be my first love, but we both know it's not yours." He raised a hand as I began to protest. "Don't see Fandango's being burned down as a problem for you. See it as an opportunity. This could be your chance to thrive."

"Away from you?"

"Explore your options. And I'm not saying any of this because I want you to go. I'd love nothing more than to have you by my side every day. But not if that's what you don't truly want deep down in your heart."

"I do want that." I swallowed around the sudden lump in my throat.

"Don't be so quick to answer. Your baking magic is troubled. You won't tell me why, and I won't push for an answer, but take time to think about what you want to do with the rest of your life."

"I... want to bake." It sounded like a question, even though I hadn't meant it to be.

"Look forward five years. If you were doing the exact same thing now in five years' time, how would you feel? Does it bring your heart joy because you're working in a new version of Fandango's?" He shook his head. "I have a feeling it wouldn't."

"You don't know that."

"I know enough to understand my wonderful niece needs more than she currently has."

"Not from you. That's your medication talking. And you're tired. Get some rest. I'll be by to see you tomorrow." I kissed his cheek, blinking away tears before he had the chance to see them.

He simply nodded. "Very well. We can talk more another time."

After a hasty goodbye, I hurried out and closed the door behind me.

My dad immediately caught hold of my arm and propelled me along the corridor. "I wanted to have a private word with you. Your mother is off getting sandwiches."

I'd hoped to have five minutes alone to process Uncle Albert's words, but my parents had a habit of never letting up when they wanted something. "What do you want to talk about?"

"You don't have to go with her. There are plenty of other options available. You're free to spread your wings and come with me. Don't let your mother guilt trip you into going with her."

"Dad, can we stop this?" I gently eased my arm out of his grip and turned to face him. "I love that you both want me to work with you. But right now, all I can think about is Uncle Albert. You're putting too much pressure on me to decide when I'm not in the right headspace."

"You're such a sweet girl, and of course, you'd think of your uncle. But don't put everyone else before yourself. You've always done that, ever since you were small. You just want to make other people happy."

"Is that such a bad thing?"

"It is, if you're missing out on other things. And you've turned down the last five invitations I sent you to spend time learning from the very best. I immersed myself in baking when I was your age. It was all I wanted to do." His gaze grew curious. "It's almost as if you don't care about baking. I can't understand why."

I bit my bottom lip. I knew the reason, but I wasn't sharing it with him. "I practice in Fandango's. I'm learning from one of the best by working with Uncle Albert. The Black bakers shouldn't be underestimated. He's excellent."

"I'm not belittling his talent. Albert is a solid baker, and the family is in the top twenty of baking dynasties, but I'm aiming to get the number one spot within the next five years, and I need you by my side to do that."

"You really don't." I'd push the family out of the baking league chart if I got involved in this fight to the top. "And what's so wrong with being in second place?"

He sighed. "It seems you've learned nothing from me. The best of the best are never second."

I turned my head, filtering out my dad's voice as I heard someone say the name Torin Magnus. A nurse and doctor stood together, looking at paperwork.

"Hold on a minute, Dad." I walked along the corridor.

"Where are you going? We have so much to discuss, and your mother will be back soon."

I pressed a finger to my lips and leaned against the wall, trying to be discreet as I listened to the conversation.

"Do you think he'll need more healing intervention?" the nurse said.

"No, but he was lucky to get out of that explosion with only an injured arm. The healing spells are holding nicely, and the bone is knitting together. Arrange for him to have a checkup, but there won't be any need for him to stay. Did he have observation?"

"Yes, we kept him overnight. Everything was satisfactory."

The doctor shook his head. "People shouldn't use magic they don't understand. He could have blown his head off."

"He got lucky he was brought here straightaway. If that injury had been left, his arm would never have fully healed, no matter how many spells we used on it."

"Good work, nurse. I'll get the paperwork signed off."

So Torin was definitely here the night Alaric got stabbed. That meant he couldn't have killed him.

"Luna, what are you doing?" Dad stepped in front of me. "What's the matter with you? You're acting strangely."

"Nothing. I just heard something interesting."

His forehead furrowed. "Village life is bad for you. It's made you sheltered. You've gotten used to living timidly and forgotten how exciting life can be. There is much more out there than local gossip."

"Dad! My life is plenty exciting enough."

"I hope you're not talking about that murder in the woods. I don't want you getting in more trouble." He gripped my shoulders. "Why stay here when you have a world of baking opportunity at your feet?"

I held in a sigh and looked over my dad's shoulder. Cole was striding toward me with a smile on his face.

"Luna, is there something you're not telling me?" my dad said. "Is there a problem with your magic? I'm sure I can help."

"No! Why would you say that?" Panic hit me like a sledgehammer. My parents couldn't know the truth about my baking magic.

"Then give me one good reason I shouldn't order you to come with me when I leave Witch Haven?"

My gaze flashed to Cole. "I'm staying because... I'm getting married."

Chapter 7

Cole timed his arrival perfectly. Just after I'd blurted out the lie about us getting hitched.

"Hey, Luna. I thought I'd check in on your uncle. How's he doing?" Cole's smile faded as his gaze flicked from me and then to my dad. "Is this a bad time?"

My dad was staring at me with his mouth open.

"No! It's a perfect time, actually. Sorry, but I've just revealed our secret." I grabbed Cole's hand. "Cole Kellam, I'd like you to meet my dad, Galahad Brimstone."

Dad snapped his jaw shut, and his gaze ran over Cole. "Why am I just learning about you?"

Cole's forehead furrowed. "I'm not sure I follow you, sir. It's good to meet you. Luna's told me—"

"You're marrying my daughter?"

"That's right! Cole, I've just told Dad we're getting married." I could barely get the words out. I was such an idiot, but I'd needed the perfect reason I couldn't leave Witch Haven, and he'd just strolled through the door.

Silence filled the corridor as Cole and my dad eyeballed each other.

"Is this true? You've asked for my daughter's hand in marriage?"

I had to take it back. Cole would think I was insane for saying we were getting married. "I... err... I should explain myself. It's not so much—"

"There's nothing to explain," Cole said. "That's right. I love your daughter, and I want to marry her. I've never met anyone quite like Luna. She never fails to surprise me."

My head jerked up. Had I heard him right? Why wasn't Cole running away because a crazy witch he'd been dating for five minutes announced they were spending the rest of their lives together?

"Yes. My daughter is unique," my dad said slowly. "But I'm still at a loss to understand the situation. I didn't even know she was in a relationship."

"It's been a whirlwind romance," I said. "But it feels like I've known Cole forever."

"Yet it still feels like there's so much we need to know about each other." He grinned at me and arched an eyebrow. "Since we're getting married, we'll have all the time in the world to do that."

I gulped. I was in so much trouble. "Of course we will."

My dad stretched out a hand. "Well, I suppose congratulations are in order. Although I would have preferred to get to know you before something this significant was embarked upon with my only child."

Cole shook my dad's hand. "I should have asked for your permission before proposing, but Luna got to me. She captured my heart, and I didn't want anyone else getting her before I did. She is quite a woman."

My dad released Cole's hand. "She is. And I'm extremely protective of her. I hope you can give Luna the privileged life she's entitled to."

"Dad! There's no need for that. Cole is trustworthy. He's a great guy. He's always looking out for me."

My dad's eyes narrowed. "You're a shifter?"

"I'm a werewolf. My dad is alpha of the Imperial pack. My mom maintains the only female led werewolf pack in the Four Counties. My brothers lead the Everpaw pack, the Black Fang pack, and the Hollow pack."

My eyes widened as he kept spreading out his impressive family tree. There really was a lot I needed to learn about Cole.

"Your mother is Morrigan Kellam?" my dad said.

"That's right, sir. I expect you've heard of her. She's something else." Pride rode through Cole's words.

"I have. People tell stories about her. And your father is no less impressive. He manages the silver mine logistics in Crystal Cove, is that correct?"

"He owns them, among other things. It keeps him busy. I rarely get to see him."

"I'm not surprised. I've met your father several times." An approving gleam entered my dad's eyes. Family names and money always impressed him.

"You see. Cole is great," I squeaked out.

Dad finally turned to me and gave a single nod. "Does your mother know about this?"

"You're the first to know. And it's not official. I mean, it is, but it's early days. We're not planning on getting married soon or having anything elaborate."

A snort of disbelief left him. "Your marriage will be elaborate."

"Dad, I'm not interested in that. I want something simple. Maybe a ceremony outdoors. Nothing over the top. We have both families to make happy."

"No daughter of mine is getting married outside. You can never control the weather."

"Then something small and intimate. And no over the top outfits. People can wear what they like. The werewolves can attend in their fur if they want to."

"Your mother wouldn't let you wear anything simple. You're her only daughter. She'll want to make sure you look stunning. And the press will want full coverage."

"Luna could wear a sack and she'd look beautiful," Cole said.

"Of course. That's not what I meant. But I'm sure she only wants to get married once, and she'll need it to be a day to remember. We all will. Now, are you sure your mother doesn't know about this? She's always keeping things from me."

"Dad, let's not get this blown out of proportion."

"I need to speak to her before she starts throwing around demands. I'll be right back." Dad nodded at Cole and strode away.

"Your dad is an interesting guy."

I was too ashamed to look at him. "He can be. I... err. We should probably talk about this."

"We should." Cole was quiet for a tense few seconds. "Well...?"

I dropped my head and groaned. "I'm so sorry. I just blurted it out. Dad was grilling me about going to work with him, and my mom had been pressuring me into working for her. Dad wouldn't stop with the questions. He was asking what was wrong and why I wanted to stay in Witch Haven. I didn't know what to say. I kept telling him I love it here. My uncle is here, my friends, you're here. Then I saw you walk through the door, and you were happy to see me, and... it just came out. Please don't hate me for dragging you into one of my family dramas."

"Maybe your subconscious is telling you something?" There was a half-smile on his face as he pulled me close.

"No! I don't want to marry you. I mean, you're great, and I love spending time with you, but you said it yourself, we're getting to know each other." I tipped my head back to look at him. "I had no idea about your family, though. You sound like a huge deal."

He shrugged. "We are. The Kellam's are number one in the werewolf hierarchy. Everyone who's furry knows our name, and they all want to be our friend or rip our throats out and challenge us for the top."

"Wow! I really have to brush up on my shifter knowledge."

"I don't know all that much about witch magical baking dynasties, so I can hardly judge you for not knowing about shifter hierarchies. And I liked it that you didn't know who I was when we met. A lot of women are interested in me for my money and connections."

"You're rich, too?"

He chuckled. "Yep. Probably wealthier than the Brimstones."

"I only want you for your muscles."

Cole kissed the top of my head. "You'll hear no complaints from me about that. But it seems your dad is aware of my connections."

"Don't mind him. He always crawls after anyone with money and influence."

"Luna, that's not kind."

I sighed. "I don't mean to sound nasty, but it's always been the thing that got him excited. Connections matter to him."

"Maybe they do, but he still cares for you. I could see that when he spoke with me. He was checking me out to make sure I was good enough for you."

"I know. My parents love me, but they show it with gifts and opportunities rather than hugs and lots of I love yous. It took a while to get used to. Maybe I'm still not used to it."

He nodded. "So... getting back to the whole marriage thing."

I instantly tensed. "Do we have to?"

"Yes. Don't you see me as your life mate?"

My mouth opened and closed several times. "I mean, I don't know."

Intensity flickered in his eyes. "You don't need to spare my feelings. If you don't see a long-term future for us, you tell me now. If I'm getting my heart broken, I need to fix a plan to get it put back together with the least amount of damage."

"Your heart would be broken if I said this relationship wasn't working out?"

"Sure it would. You keep forgetting, I'm a werewolf. We love hard, and we love forever. We find a mate, and that's it for us. My head won't ever get turned now I have you."

My breathing came out uneven. "Not ever?"

"No. I knew the moment I smelled you that there was something special about you."

"The moment you... smelled me?" My nose wrinkled. "That's not what I was expecting you to say."

He grinned. "The night we chased that scumbag, Bram, the air was alive. I've never smelled anything like it before. It was sweet but also fiery and spicy. You charged the atmosphere as you moved through it. You were fearless the way you chased that guy down."

"If I remember rightly, you actually chased him down."

"I lent a helping paw. And I couldn't resist. You drew me into the fight. I knew I was meant to protect you and be with you for the rest of my life."

My heart raced. "Going back a step. When you find your mate, is that really it for you? I'm your life mate, not just someone you're having fun with?"

The expression that crossed his face had my pulse stuttering. It was a mixture of fear and determination. "That's exactly what I meant. I'm dedicated to you and only you. Since that first moment we met, I knew you were the one for me."

"Is that how it works with werewolves?"

"That's the way it works."

"Even though I chained you up in my farmhouse and got your leg broken when you were stalking me? None of that changed how you feel?"

"I was mad for a time, but that happens in all relationships. And sometimes, the bonding process makes no sense. Werewolves sometimes fall for a mate who seems to be their tormentor when they first get together. But it's something deep inside us that knows. And it's always right." His thumb traced across my cheekbone. "Of course, it makes it tricky when we bond with someone who's not a werewolf, because they don't have the same responses. I need to find a way to get you to fall in love with me and never stop falling."

I was finding it increasingly hard to breathe. "You plan to make me fall in love with you forever?"

"I do. Because if I can't figure that out, then I'm lost. No one would ever fill that gap. When I look into my future, I only see you. It has to be you."

If there was ever a moment to swoon, this was it. I didn't know what to say, so I simply wrapped my arms around Cole's broad chest and held him close. Could I really marry this incredible guy for real? My heart said hell yes, but my head was in shock that this hadn't backfired.

Cole ran his fingers through my hair. "I love the prospect of marrying you, but I wouldn't mind getting the chance to ask you. I know you're a modern woman, but I'd like to get down on one knee at some point and do it the right way."

I leaned back and stared up at him. "You're incredible. You've always been honest with me. I've never met anyone like you."

His grin was like a warm summer's day after a month of snow. "You're open to a proposal from me?"

I laughed. "Of course. But don't think I'm pressuring you into anything. There's no rush."

"It would have happened. Sure, maybe we'd have spent a few months getting to know each other, but I already know enough about you to know I am all in. I just didn't want to rush you and scare you off. Your life isn't easy. You're dealing with a lot of tricky business."

I nodded slowly. "I am. But I'd love a way to un-complicate things. And I'd love a future with you. That part feels easy and right."

"Then let's make that happen." Cole was just leaning down to kiss me, when there was a shriek, and I jumped back.

"Why didn't you tell me?" My mom rushed toward us.

I untangled myself from Cole and was almost knocked off my feet as she hugged me. "Mom! Calm down."

She cupped my face in her hands. "A wedding! You're really getting married? All the charming young men I've suggested for you, and you turned them all down. Is this the reason?"

"Um..." I nodded. "Mom, meet Cole. Cole, this is Cloris Brimstone."

My mom turned and embraced Cole. "I've been hearing all about you from my husband. This is wonderful news. I want to know everything, and you must tell me about the proposal. I hope it was romantic."

Cole grinned at me as he stepped back from my mom's embrace. "It's a pleasure to meet you. We were just talking about the proposal."

"I have so many thoughts in my head that it's hard to get them in order. Where should we start?" my mom said. "We must talk venues first. They get booked so far in advance. Do you want a beach wedding? Or I know several castles that could be available. What about a manor house? That would be wonderful. We have to pick somewhere with plenty of green space for the photographs. And of course, it'll need to be a spring or summer wedding so we can guarantee good weather. Oh! And the dress."

"Mom, slow down. We'll have plenty of time to organize everything. Cole will also want a say in the wedding plans. It's not just down to you."

He lifted a hand. "I know not to tread on toes."

"Men never want to be involved in weddings," my mom said.

"I want to be involved. I'm making the wedding cake." My dad strode along the corridor toward us. He glared at my mom. "You said you were using the washroom."

"I changed my mind. And you can't make the wedding cake. Luna's my daughter. I must make her cake."

"No! I'll do a better job of the wedding cake. I made Princess Aurelia's cake. That was in the society pages for weeks after it was presented to the bride and groom."

"Yes, but I made the cake for—"

"Stop!" I moved in between my parents before they started a physical fight over cake baking responsibilities. "Nothing's been decided about a single thing related to the wedding. Maybe I'll make my own wedding cake, or I'll ask Uncle Albert to do it."

"I must make it," my dad said.

"If you keep arguing, I'll buy it off the shelf." I glared at him.

Both parents spluttered about that suggestion, but at least it stopped them from bickering for a few seconds.

"I want to make something special for your day," my mom said, "a wedding cake to remember."

"My cake would be just as memorable. Don't feel pressured into doing anything your mother wants."

"I'm being pressured by both of you, and it's not fair. This is between me and Cole." I sighed at the stricken looks on their faces. "Of course, I'd love your input into the wedding, but ultimately, the decisions will be made by us."

Tabitha hurried along the corridor toward us. "Sorry to interrupt. We've had bad news."

I whirled around. "It's not Uncle Albert, is it?"

"No, he's fine. But because of the continued bad weather, the hospital is at risk of flooding. We've called in reinforcements to deal with the torrential rain, but the elemental witches are dealing with other emergencies in the village."

I hadn't noticed it had begun to pour again, but when I looked out a window, the rain was hammering down. "Can we help?"

"I hope so. All non-emergency patients are being immediately discharged, including Albert. Are you able to take him? He can't be left alone overnight. Someone will need to watch him."

"Of course. We'll figure something out," I said.

"I've already packed his things, so he's almost ready to go." Tabitha glanced around then passed me a piece of paper. She leaned in close. "I hope you don't think this is inappropriate, but these are my contact details. I wasn't brave enough to give them to Albert, but I'd love to see him when he's not a patient. He's such a charming man."

I grinned as I tucked away the information. "I'm sure he'd love that too. I'll see what I can do to make it happen."

She grinned before dashing away to inform other visitors about the flooding.

"Let's get Albert out of here," my mom said.

Dad nodded and followed her.

I was glad the flooding news had temporarily stopped them from fighting, but they'd soon prime their icing bags for round two of who got to make my wedding cake.

Rolling my shoulders, I let out a sigh. This was only the beginning of wedding cake wars.

Cole was smiling at me, and I rolled my eyes in response. He shouldn't be so happy. He'd just agreed to have the most demanding in-laws you'd ever meet.

I made a quick call to Odessa to see if she could squeeze in one more guest. I started smiling, too. Things were looking up in the love department for Uncle Albert and me.

If only I could get my parents to stop fighting and someone hadn't been killed with one of my knives, life really would be great.

Chapter 8

"Have you thought what colors you want?" Mom sat at Odessa's kitchen table.

I gritted my teeth and turned away from the kitchen sink, a forced smile on my face. "There's more to life than planning my wedding."

"Not for me. This is the most important catering event I'll ever look after. Forget about all the kings, queens, and celebrities I've worked for. You're my daughter, and I plan to make this perfect."

"Nothing is ever perfect, but I appreciate your interest. Just take it easy on the mother of the bride possessed by an evil wedding planner act, or you'll scare away Cole."

Mom didn't object to my description of her. "I see by the way he looks at you that nothing would scare him off."

"Let's not test that theory. He's a great guy, but I'm sure you could push him too far." I set down the dishcloth and dried my hands. Odessa had been kind enough to invite not only Uncle Albert to stay but also my parents, so they could move out of the bed-and-breakfast they'd been staying in. All her bedrooms were full, and the treasure hunters had spent the night in one of Odessa's barns after she'd cleared it of scarecrows.

Mom glanced out the window. "We have little time until your father gets back. We need to get things sorted."

I tilted my head. "What's going on with you two? Why can't you both make my wedding cake?"

She peered into her coffee mug. "Our magic doesn't blend well."

"It does. You've been married forever. It has to blend well."

Her fingers tightened around the mug. "These days, we work differently. Your father can be very bossy."

"Mom, he's not the only one who can be bossy. That's sort of why you work so well."

She sighed. "But I always imagined I'd be the one who made your cake when the time came. He's only muscling in because he knows the publicity it'll get."

"Not that again. My wedding won't be a publicity event. I don't mind friends and family taking pictures, but I want nothing sold to the society pages. If you want to send a small picture and an announcement, then fair enough, but that's it. This isn't turning into a spectacle."

"Darling, this wedding will be the making of you. And two incredible families are uniting. It might even get more business from the werewolves. We could branch out."

I glowered at her. "Neither is this wedding a business opportunity. It's about love."

We'd been having variations of this conversation all morning and most of yesterday afternoon after getting back from the hospital, and I was exhausted. I had a tension headache and desperately needed a break.

"Oh, I think that's your father coming back." Mom frowned at the closed kitchen door. "Odessa was most insistent he look at her scarecrows. She must have forgotten he's not an outdoorsy type."

I pressed my lips together. She'd been insistent because I'd begged her to get rid of him for a bit so I could have some peace. But the second he'd left, Mom had stepped into the breach and attacked, all confetti guns blazing, to get me on side when it came to the wedding.

Dad strode in with Odessa beside him. "It's a most impressive business. And the spice you use in that pumpkin bread is incredible."

Odessa grinned and slid me a discreet wink. "It's my secret blend. It's what makes all my muffins and pancakes so special."

"I'd be interested in discussing a franchise opportunity with you. It would sell well in a number of upmarket venues."

She shook her head. "I mainly keep it for personal use and share it with a few special people. I don't want to get overwhelmed with orders. I've got enough on my hands with the scarecrows and pumpkins. And I've already got an ad out to hire an assistant because I'm so busy."

"I'd offer generous terms. You'd get a decent cut of the profits." Dad accepted a mug of coffee from Odessa as she bustled around the kitchen.

"Dad, Odessa's not interested." I looked at her. "Don't let him pressure you. When he wants something, he never gives up until he gets it."

Odessa giggled. "It's fine. People always react like that around my pumpkin spice. I've learned dozens of ways to say no politely."

I checked the time. "I need to take lunch over to the campers."

The treasure hunters had returned to their camp after they'd heard from Devlin that it was no longer off-limits. They'd gone to gather their equipment but intended to spend the day there and asked for food to be brought over. Since I'd been paid upfront for the job, I was happy to oblige.

"But we've got so much to talk about," my mom said.

"We can talk about it tonight. You focus on looking after Uncle Albert. I won't be long." I'd take as long as I could. A break from all the wedding pressure was in order.

Odessa helped me load up a basket of food. "Do you want me to come with you? I could drive."

I shook my head. "Thanks, but I could do with a walk." Plus, I planned to make a quick stop at my hidden farmhouse. I'd spent barely any time with my magic harem since the bakery fire, and they must feel neglected.

"I'll keep your parents entertained. We can talk about your wedding." Odessa gave me a pointed look.

I grimaced. "Ah. About that. Sorry for not saying anything to you. It's been a shock for me, too."

She glanced at my parents. "We can discuss it another time. But we will talk about it. You've been holding out on me. That's not what friends do."

"I promise, we will."

I waved a quick goodbye and hurried out of the farmhouse, grabbed the extra supplies I'd stashed outside for my harem, and dashed to the woods. I hurried along the trail, lowered the magic barrier that concealed the farmhouse, and stepped through.

Only when the barrier was in place did I let out a huge sigh, and the tension left my shoulders. My parents were full on, and I wasn't sure how much longer I'd cope with having them around. I loved them, but sometimes, I didn't like them all that much.

I headed into the farmhouse, calling out a loud hello. I walked into the front parlor to find Gloria, Faye, and Ridley in there.

"What have you got us?" Gloria said. "You've brought a bounty by the looks of it."

"Only one basket is for you." I set it down, and Ridley pulled it open. "I've got to go to a campsite in the woods and feed the hungry hordes. And I've got a lot to tell you."

They listened in rapt attention as I told them about my parents' visit, what happened to the treasure hunters, and even the surprise wedding announcement. I left nothing out. They were often starved of information and appreciated it when I gave them a thorough rundown of the local gossip. And this was quite some gossip.

Ridley frowned. "You're really getting married to him?"

I smiled. Ridley had a tiny crush on me, but it was more out of necessity than us being perfect for each other. He was lonely, and a young, good-looking guy. He needed a girlfriend. "It looks like it."

"You barely know him."

"But Cole knows Luna," Gloria said. "I've been around a few werewolves in my time, and when they know they've found the one, that's it for them."

I nodded. "That's what Cole said. And it was a huge surprise. I didn't realize he was so interested in me."

"Do you love him?" Gloria said. "Werewolves can be surly and intimidating on the outside, but they have tender hearts. And when they give it away, that's it for them. They can't take it back. If you're not sure about Cole, you must let him down now. He won't be able to do anything about the bond he has with you, but werewolves have other ways of dealing with a broken heart."

"I... do love him." It was the first time I'd said that. "It's so new, though, that it's scary. But what do you mean, werewolves have other ways of fixing a broken heart?"

"He'd get a new wife," Ridley muttered. "You should stick with me."

Gloria tutted. "I didn't say fixing. A werewolf who loses the love of his life becomes a kamikaze wolf. They're unstable and not safe to be around, so they get sent on suicide missions or given jobs they're not expected to survive for long."

My stomach clenched, and I felt queasy. "I'd never want that for Cole. I'll make sure he knows how I feel. I think he does. We're figuring things out."

"I guess, so long as he makes you happy, I shouldn't complain about you getting hitched," Ridley said.

"I am happy. And I haven't forgotten about you. I know you want company."

He shrugged. "I'm used to hanging out with these old girls. I even had a dirty dream about Faye the other night."

Faye's cheeks flushed. "Don't be ridiculous. What happened in your dream?"

Ridley laughed and tapped the side of his nose.

"I'm thrilled you're getting married, Luna," Gloria said. "It's just a shame we won't be able to come to the wedding."

"It is. But I'll bring you all slices of cake, providing my parents agree on who's making it."

"We could go in disguise," Faye said. "We wouldn't stop for long, just for the ceremony. Oh! That's if we're invited. We are invited, aren't we?"

"I'd love for you all to be there. We can figure something out. But there are hundreds of things to plan first. And if my parents get their way, I won't be involved in any of it."

"You do what feels right for you and Cole," Gloria said. "Don't be pushed around by anyone. Weddings can easily get out of control."

"And before the wedding, I want to focus on Alaric's murder. It's wrong someone used my knife to kill such a gentle guy."

"Do you really think it was another treasure hunter who stabbed him?" Gloria said.

"I like lavender," Faye said.

"For what?"

"Your color theme for the wedding."

"We've moved on from the werewolf wedding," Ridley grumbled.

"I haven't. Lavender and white. Don't do red and white, though. That's blood and tears, which is a bad omen. I like the idea of something simple and outdoors, though."

I nodded. "Me, too. And I'd love to have the wedding in the village, but my parents are already trying to convince me to leave Witch Haven. With this new murder, they don't think it's a safe place to be."

"You won't, will you?" Gloria grabbed my hand and squeezed tight. "You won't leave us?"

"Never. I'm staying here, and so are you. My parents can push all they like, but this is my home."

"We'd be lost without you," Faye said. "And we really would love to see you and Cole get married, but we won't be able to travel. It's too risky."

"I'll convince my parents Witch Haven is the perfect place for a wedding and for me and Cole to set up home for good."

"So you're going to solve this murder to prove to them it's not a dangerous place to live?" Ridley said.

"That's the plan. And it should be easy. The remaining treasure hunters are all at the camp, and I'm heading over there after this visit. I figured I'd chat with them and see if anyone seems suspicious."

"Be careful. If one of them has found the gem, they'll be unstoppable. You don't want to die before your wedding," Faye said.

"I don't want to die at all, but I'll be careful. And the gem isn't real, so no one could have it."

"I've heard things about that gem," Gloria said. "Don't be so sure it doesn't exist."

"I've heard rumors about it too, but have you ever seen it?" I said.

"No, but the legend goes back many hundreds of years. It's been written about in all kinds of old books."

"That still doesn't mean it's real," Ridley said. "Why don't you take your werewolf fiancé with you and he can look after you?"

"Ridley, don't be jealous. I'd take you with me if I could."

He grumbled but seemed placated when I kissed his cheek.

"I'd better get going. The treasure hunters are waiting for their lunch. I'll be back soon, but I've got a lot on my hands, what with the bakery, Uncle Albert recovering from his burns, and my parents hounding my every step."

"And the wedding," Faye said.

"And the murder," Ridley said.

"Yes, to both. There's fresh food in the basket for several days. That'll see you right."

"So long as Ridley doesn't eat it all now." Gloria pulled a packet of cookies away from him and swatted the back of his hand.

"And if you get desperate, there's dried and tinned goods in the cellar."

"You get on, focus on your family. We'll be fine," Gloria said. "I've got several complicated knitting patterns to get on with, and Ridley's on level twelve of his game. That keeps him busy."

"Level fifteen, actually." Ridley puffed up his chest.

"I'm glad you won't get bored."

"Would you like a little magic boost while you're here?" Faye wriggled her fingers at me.

"I wouldn't mind. I won't take much." I'd been careful around my magic harem ever since making Ridley collapse the last time I'd drained him of magic.

Thirty minutes later, with a boost of magic from them all, I left the farmhouse and headed to the campsite, which was a twenty-minute brisk walk along worn tracks.

The going underfoot was slippery thanks to the torrential rain making the paths muddy, but I was glad for some alone time. Dealing with a murder, my parents, and now a wedding was a lot to process. Eek! I was getting married.

I was almost at the campsite, when the air warmed around me. I yelped as Storm and Indigo appeared in front of me, blocking my path.

"Hey! You scared me half to death. What are you doing here?"

"You're getting hitched to a werewolf and didn't think to tell us," Storm said.

Indigo arched an eyebrow. "What's going on?"

"Oh! I..." I had no explanation, other than I was a terrible friend.

"Couldn't be bothered to tell your oldest friends you were getting married?" Storm glowered at me.

"No, it's not that." I set down the basket. "It was sudden and unexpected. We decided to get married last night at the hospital."

"Just like that?" Indigo said. "You haven't mentioned anything about getting married to Cole. Why the rush?"

Storm's gaze settled on my stomach. "Are you pregnant?"

"No!"

"Not that it would matter if you were, but I'd want a chat with your furry friend about safety measures in the bedroom." Storm pursed her lips. "Maybe I should have that talk with you, too."

"It's definitely not because of a baby. I was going to tell you as soon as I could."

"Yet we had to hear about it from Odessa, who's also not happy with you, although she'd never tell you that."

"You don't want me to marry Cole?"

"Marry who you like," Indigo said. "I mean, so long as we approve. But you should have told us what was going on."

I didn't miss the flicker of hurt in my best friend's eyes. "I'm sorry. There's been so much happening that I messed up. The bakery fire, Uncle Albert in the hospital, Alaric's murder, my parents showing up and taking over. I lost track of things. I would have told you. And I want you involved in the wedding. I'd love it if you'd both be my bridesmaids. Odessa, too."

"I'm not wearing some over the top dress with ruffles," Storm said.

"You won't have to. I haven't figured out any details yet, but I want you all involved. You have to be there."

The frowns on their faces remained in place. I had some making up to do, and the offer of floaty dresses wasn't cutting it.

Neither of them said anything, but their unhappy glares spoke volumes.

My mouth twisted to the side. "This situation is complicated."

Storm smirked. "That's your whole life, hidden under a fragile veneer of everything is fine."

I winced. "I've just had an unlucky run lately. I'm not that bad."

"You're also not that good," Indigo said. "And what are you doing out here? I figured the location spell I cast went wonky when it directed us to the woods."

"She's probably burying secrets she doesn't want us to find," Storm muttered.

"I don't have any secrets." I had loads of secrets, and they were all at risk of tumbling out if I wasn't careful.

Indigo sighed and shook her head. "Have you seen those crazy storm clouds? You shouldn't be out in the woods when it's about to pour again. You'll get stuck."

"I'm topping up the food for the treasure hunters. They came back here to collect their gear this morning. I'll be five minutes. You can come with me if you like. I can't hang around, or the food will spoil." I hurried past before they could continue their interrogation. I felt terrible not letting them know about my engagement to Cole, but with the shock of everything that happened last night, it had slipped my mind.

After a few seconds, I heard them following me.

"There's something you're still not telling us," Storm said.

My pace increased. "There is?"

"Why did Cole propose to you in the hospital?"

"I proposed to him, sort of."

"You did?" Indigo said. "You haven't known him long. Are you sure you're not pregnant? You spent the night together at the library."

"When he had a broken leg! There was no hanky panky." I shrugged. "Besides, I'm a modern woman. I can ask a guy to marry me if I want to."

They caught up with me and positioned themselves on either side of me. It felt like I was being trapped so I couldn't escape further questioning.

"What made you suddenly ask him, though?" Indigo said.

"It felt like the right time. I saw Cole, and he looked so handsome, and my parents were pressuring me for a good reason to stay in Witch Haven—"

"Wait! They want you to leave?"

"They do. They said, now Fandango's is gone, Uncle Albert can retire and I can join one of them. They're fighting over who I go with, and it's not pretty. I'm doing my best to keep out of their way until things calm down."

"Odessa said your parents were being intense. Do you want to go with them?" Storm said.

"No. I'm staying here, not that they believe me. Anyway, Dad was trying to force me into saying I'd go with him. Then Cole came along, so I said we were getting married."

Storm tipped back her head and roared a laugh. "You used Cole as an excuse to stay? The marriage proposal isn't real?"

"It is! And he's not an excuse. I like the guy. And he loves me. He did the whole werewolf declaration thing last night. Honestly, it terrified me. I had no idea he was that serious about the relationship. I thought he'd hear me say the word marriage and race away, but he's all in. So... we're getting married."

"Werewolf mate bonds are so weird," Storm said.

Indigo slung an arm around my shoulders. "You're a hot, wonderful mess. You're marrying this guy just to get away from your parents."

"No, I'm really not. Sure, it's super early in the relationship to talk marriage, but it makes sense. And we'd have gotten there, eventually. Most likely."

"You'll only make things worse if you keep lying to your parents."

"I'm not lying. And I'm also not leaving Witch Haven. Plus, there's this murder to sort out."

"This gets better. You're involved in that, too?" Storm said.

"No! At least, only my knife was involved. It's the murder weapon."

Storm chuckled, and Indigo groaned.

"You've got to stop shutting us out of your dramas," Indigo said. "We might help you get out of these messes, but you just keep digging a big hole and throwing in more complications."

"Not deliberately. Come on, let's get to the camp. I'll offload this food, and then we can go back to Odessa's farmhouse and talk about the wedding."

"I can't stick around for much longer." Storm checked her watch. "Work's busy."

"And I'm meeting Olympus in an hour. But we will learn all about your proposal, wedding plans, and exactly what's going on with you soon," Indigo said.

"I can't wait."

We arrived in the clearing, and I was surprised to see most of the tents still standing, although Alaric's had been disassembled.

I raised a hand when Torin emerged from the other side of the clearing, still with his arm in a sling.

He lifted his chin in acknowledgement and strode toward me.

Something huge and fast caught my attention. I froze to the spot, too shocked to move. It was a boulder, and it was rocketing straight at Torin's head.

Chapter 9

I dropped the basket, raised my hands, and blasted out a spell. I had no idea what I was sending at that boulder, but all I knew was I had to destroy it before it killed Torin.

His eyes widened as he saw me aiming magic at his head and threw himself to the dirt. A second later, a huge bolt of lightning blasted from my chest and smashed the boulder into tiny pieces, scattering it around the clearing.

I lowered my hands and rasped out a breath, the burn from the magic pulsing through me in a hot wave.

"Wow! That was one heck of a spell." Indigo stared at me. "I didn't know you could do that."

"What was that?" Elsa raced into the clearing, Reuben on her heels.

Torin was still face down in the dirt, covered in a fine layer of tiny pieces of boulder. He lifted his head.

I hurried over and helped him up. "Are you okay?"

He blinked several times but nodded. "I think so. What happened?"

"I saw the boulder," Reuben said. "I don't know where it came from, but it was heading straight for you."

I nodded. "Sorry to scare you by shooting magic your way, but it would have squashed you flat."

Torin looked at the mess on the ground. "A boulder? I can't believe it. How did it roll? There aren't any big hills nearby."

Storm tugged my elbow. "Where did you get that kind of power?"

"I didn't even realize what I was doing. I didn't think of the spell to use, just stared at the boulder and focused my magic on destroying it."

"Huh!" Storm placed her hands on her hips as she studied me like I was a curiosity under a microscope.

"Are you sure you're okay?" I said to Torin.

"Yeah, thanks to you."

"Have we had enough warnings now?" Elsa said.

Indigo turned to her. "What are you talking about?"

"We should leave. It's this gem curse. It wants us all dead. First, Torin was hurt, then Alaric got stabbed, and now this."

Torin nodded slowly. "I didn't believe in the curse, but after everything that's happened to me, how many hints does a guy need?"

"But we were going to stay here a couple more nights," Reuben said. "We've paid for the full week. And we must be close to finding the gem if the curse is getting twitchy."

"You can stay if you like," Torin said. "The curse isn't interested in you."

"Or maybe it's picking us off one at a time," Elsa whispered.

I studied Reuben carefully. Nothing bad had happened to him or Elsa. Could they be behind Alaric's murder and Torin's injury? They were getting rid of the competition, so there'd be fewer people to share the gem's power with.

"Torin, are you sure the explosion in the cave was just your magic misfiring?" I said.

He brushed boulder dust off his clothes. "That's what I initially thought. I was using old potions I'd mixed years ago. I figured they'd be fine if I shook them and gave them a refresh."

"Don't forget you smelt something strange in the cave just before the explosion," Elsa said.

He nodded. "I did, but I dismissed it. I was so keen on finding the gem. We are close, but death feels closer."

"It's why the curse is so active," Elsa said. "It senses how near we are to getting our hands on that gem and wants to stop us."

"Which is why we should keep looking! Once we have the gem, the curse can suck eggs. It won't be able to touch us," Reuben said.

"No. We should all leave," Torin said. "The longer we spend here, the more likely someone else will die. And I'm at the top of the list."

"You really think the curse killed that other guy?" Storm said.

Torin glanced at her. "I do. And you are?"

I quickly made the introductions. "Odessa said you're welcome to stay in her barn for as long as you like. And you probably want to stick around until the Magic Council figures out what happened to Alaric, don't you?"

"It's good of her to offer, but those scarecrows freaked me out. There were several creeping around the barn last night. I was certain they were trying to get to us," Torin said.

"Don't worry about the scarecrows. They only attack when Odessa tells them to," I said.

Torin snorted a disbelieving laugh. "I would like to find out what happened to Alaric, but this is the second time I've almost been killed. If I'm sticking around, I'm demanding protection."

"Where will you get protection from?" I said.

"The Magic Council. We could all be at risk from this curse, and they've done nothing to help us."

"That's because they're investigating what really happened," Storm said. "Solving your friend's murder is more important to them than looking after you because you can't protect yourself."

Torin shot her a filthy glare. "I can protect myself just fine, but this curse is focused on me. If Luna hadn't been here just now, I'd be dead. This feels targeted and personal. We've angered the curse. I'm demanding protection, or I'm leaving Witch Haven." He turned and strode away.

"Err... is that our lunch?" Reuben nodded at the basket I'd dropped.

"Oh, sure. That's what I came to deliver." It seemed the threat of a killer curse looming over his head hadn't squashed his appetite.

"We could do with a break," Elsa said. "We've spent ages clearing up, taking down Alaric's tent, and storing his things. The Magic Council didn't exactly leave this place tidy when they searched it."

"And since Torin's stormed off, you're welcome to stay and eat his share," Reuben said.

Storm nudged Indigo. "I need to get out of here. You can stay if you like."

"I think we're done." She gave me a piercing look. "We'll talk later."

"Oh, sure." That was something to look forward to. "I'll catch up with you another time."

They nodded a goodbye to Elsa and Reuben and walked away.

We moved to the shelter of some trees, and I unpacked the food. Reuben dragged over three upturned logs, and we sat on them while Elsa dug out bottles of water.

"Torin seems really shaken up," I said.

Elsa handed me a bottle of water. "I would be too if the curse was after me."

"It's a shame our adventure has gone wrong. And it was Torin's idea to do this treasure hunt." Reuben selected several cheese and ham sandwiches and settled them on his khaki covered knee.

"I thought Alaric was the brains of this expedition," I said.

"Sure, he was the clever one, but Torin's the organizer. Alaric did the background research and gathered the information, and he even helped pinpoint this location. He was convinced the gem was here." Elsa took a bite of sandwich. "There's a network of narrow underground tunnels beneath our feet. It seems like the perfect location for storing such an incredible object."

"I know about a few caves around here, but I didn't know about the tunnels. Are you sure about that?"

Reuben nodded as he munched on a sandwich. "They're down there. Not many people know about them because they were wiped off the maps about a hundred and fifty years ago. It's almost as if whoever did that didn't want anyone else to find them. I wonder why that is? Could it be because there's a rare and powerful gem beneath our feet?"

"Did Alaric find a map showing you these tunnels and where the gem could be found?"

He grinned. "If only it was that easy. Alaric discovered a fragment of an old map showing part of the tunnels. It had been burned, so I guess whoever incinerated it didn't want anyone else to know about them."

"Could it have been the person who hid the gem?"

"That's what we thought," Elsa said. "But now we'll never know. The map doesn't show the entire tunnel section, so we only had part of it to go on. The plan was to travel underground as far as we could and then remap the network. We'd rule out all the tunnels until we found the spot where the gem had been placed."

"That was the theory, but it could have taken us months to complete that work," Reuben said. "Who knows how far those tunnels go?"

"They could lead to the village," I said. "Maybe they were underground escape routes. There have been periods in history when not everyone was kind to magic users. It would have been a way to get from the village and into the safety of the woods."

"These woods aren't safe," Reuben said. "I keep getting the sense we're being watched."

"By the curse?" Elsa jerked her head around.

"I doubt it's the curse, but you probably are being watched. The creatures in these woods are intensely curious. Most don't bite or abduct you unless you anger them, though," I said.

Elsa shook her head. "I thought this would be a game, going gem hunting. I felt like a female Indiana Jones. Now, I'll be grateful if I get out of here in one piece."

"We'll make it out. Some dumb curse won't get us," Reuben said. "We should keep looking."

Elsa grumbled her unhappiness as she grabbed more food.

"Have you heard anything from the Magic Council about what happened to Alaric?" I asked.

"So far, nothing useful," Reuben said. "The guy investigating, Devlin something, he said any useful evidence was washed away when the bad weather set in. They took away Alaric's body to see if they can find anything on it, but he didn't seem hopeful."

"He questioned us again, but I remember little about that night. I shouldn't have had so much to drink. If I hadn't been tipsy, I might have heard Alaric cry out for help. We could have stopped whoever attacked him."

Neither of them spoke as they continued to eat, glum expressions on their faces.

"Did Alaric have enemies? Anyone holding a grudge who could track him out here? It's an isolated spot, so it's a great place to kill someone."

Elsa shuddered. "He never talked much about anything other than his research and his interest in magic relics. I don't think he had many friends, so I'm assuming he had no enemies. He was just a sweet, nerdy guy with a passion for history and legends. I can't see how that would have gathered enemies over the years."

"Unless someone else wanted the gem," Reuben said. "We only ever had private conversations online or in secure group chats, but maybe someone hacked the information. They could have found out what we were doing, got worried Alaric was getting too close, so snuck in the camp."

We all took a moment to look around, and I had a creeping sensation of being watched. But the more I thought about it, the more certain I was the killer was in this camp.

"Without Alaric, I can't see how we'll ever find this gem," Elsa said.

"I think we should still try." Reuben downed his water.

"The tunnel routes he'd plotted out were damaged in the rain. All the information got smudged. We shouldn't stay," Elsa said. "There's no point in risking our lives for something we'll never find."

"As I said, you're welcome at Odessa's farmhouse. I know the scarecrows can be intense, but they're excellent guards. If anyone was coming after you, they'd stop them."

"Thanks, that's not a bad idea. We can finish up here, then go back to the farmhouse," Elsa said. "And despite Torin throwing a fit about leaving,

Devlin doesn't want us to go anywhere until this matter is resolved."

"Because he thinks one of us did it," Reuben grumbled.

"Of course he's going to think that. We're the only ones here who knew Alaric, and they always look at those closest to the victim first. Anyone who watches TV dramas knows that."

"But we were here!" Reuben pointed to the clearing. "And we saw nothing."

Elsa shrugged and looked away. "Because we were too busy getting drunk."

"I'd better get back," I said. "I'll serve dinner at the farmhouse tonight. You can eat with all of us if you like. You're more than welcome to join us inside."

"Thanks. We'd appreciate the company," Elsa said. "And thanks for bringing our lunch out here."

"You're welcome. And it's what you're paying me for. Try not to worry about the curse. I know you'd love to find this gem, but maybe it's time to give up the hunt. Some things really aren't worth dying for."

They both grunted their agreement as I left them to enjoy their last meal in the forest.

I'd just left the clearing, when there was a blast of brilliant blue light, and a fairy appeared. Her forehead was furrowed, her tiny hands clenched into fists, and her glossy pink lips pursed.

"Don't take another step, Luna Brimstone. We have a problem."

Chapter 10

"Rainbow! What are you doing out here?" I made sure to keep safely away from the tiny cascades of glitter that drifted from the PR whiz's fluttering wings. People wrongly assumed that because fairies were small, they couldn't do much harm. The opposite was true, and their glitter felt like tiny daggers digging into your skin if you were unlucky enough to be covered in the stuff.

Her cute button nose wrinkled, and her purple eyes flashed with anger. "I've heard rumors you're telling everyone our mystical gem isn't real." Her wings beat faster.

I backed away from the glitter shower. "I... um, I might have said that to one or two people."

"Why do that? The legendary Witch Haven treasure isn't to be sullied by cynical locals. It's a tourism gold mine."

"Someone is dead because of their obsession with finding that gem. I won't encourage their friends to stay and risk getting hurt."

Rainbow fluttered a hand in the air. "That murder had nothing to do with the gem."

I crossed my arms over my chest. "Alaric was obsessed with finding it. That's the reason he was here. Perhaps he got too close and someone silenced him. If people get murdered when visiting Witch Haven, it won't do your visitor numbers any good."

A tiny snort of anger shot from Rainbow's nose. "That gem is a tourist draw. Have you any idea how much money it makes for the village?"

"No, and I don't care. A man is dead, and another one was almost seriously injured today."

Her nose wrinkled again. "I've not heard about this. Why haven't I been told?"

"It's only just happened. Sorry, Rainbow, but I don't have time right now. Torin, the guy who was almost killed, has gone to report it to the Magic Council. You work for them. I'm sure you can find the report when it gets filed." I tried to move past her, but she spun around my head so fast I grew dizzy.

"Tell me what's going on. This could be an opportunity."

"To publicize how dangerous it is to search for the gem?"

"No, foolish witch! People love a dash of danger and mystery. This is a dream story. And murder always draws a crowd. Who doesn't love to stare at a dead body or the location of some gruesome slaying?"

"Me. And I doubt Torin thought almost getting crushed was a dream."

She hovered in front of my face, a gleam of delight entering her eyes. "We must make use of this."

"You can do what you like, but I'm encouraging the remaining treasure hunters to leave as soon as possible."

She tsked at me. "This proves there are powerful magic wards in place protecting the gem, which makes it even more real to my wonderfully gullible tourists. I anticipate a twelve percent increase in visitors attempting to find the gem thanks to this incident."

"I'm sure those figures will impress Torin. He'll be glad his injuries haven't been for nothing."

"I'm impressed by the potential for a great story." Rainbow jabbed a finger at me. "You must stop putting people off from visiting Witch Haven to find the gem. It's a key tourist draw."

"Find something else to lure them here. I don't want people to waste their time or risk death!"

"Tourists bringing their money to the village isn't a waste of time. And since Fandango's makes a healthy turnover thanks to those visitors, you should do everything you can to encourage this situation."

"I'd rather not profit from murder."

Rainbow squeaked. "This is business."

"I need to go. Uncle Albert got out of the hospital last night, and I want to make sure he's doing okay."

"I'll come with you." Rainbow fluttered along beside me. "How's the bakery situation?"

"It's still burnt to the ground. There is no bakery."

"There must be. Fandango's has always been an excellent tourist attraction. It needs to be reopened as soon as possible."

"I can't help you with that. The fire is still being investigated. I've yet to get the final report from Mitchell, but it's looking like arson. That means Magic Council involvement and potentially lots of hoops to jump through to get the insurance money."

"Which is unfortunate, but you must find a temporary fix. People need their treats from the bakery. I've already dealt with several unhappy visitors who were unable to buy from you. It was most troublesome."

"We can hardly rebuild the place in a week."

She swatted me with a wing. "Think more laterally. What about the empty store next door to the bakery? Did that get any damage in the fire?"

"No. Just ours by the looks of things."

"There's your solution. Use that store. It was suitable for the Bewitching Bakery Showdown, so I'm sure you can make use of it to serve your treats."

"I'm not so sure. Uncle Albert's hands were injured in the fire, and he's still recovering. He won't be baking anything for a while."

She glanced at my hands. "Yours appear to be functioning fine. You do the baking."

"That won't work. We're taking a break from running a business. My parents are here, and—"

"I didn't know they were visiting. You should have told me." She thumped me with her wing again.

I winced and rubbed the back of my head. Were those things made of steel?

"I must organize exclusive interviews with Galahad and Cloris. I've been hearing wonderful things about the cake your father made for the Duchess Briarforest."

"You can try. They're staying at Odessa Grimsbane's farmhouse." It would be good to give them something else to think about, and it would get them out from under my feet. Dad was never one to turn down publicity opportunities.

She made a noise of disgust. "That place! I avoid going there. One of Odessa's hooligan scarecrows tried to rip off one of my wings. I had to beat him into the dirt before he let go."

"Maybe he thought you were being a nuisance."

"As if. But here's an idea. Your parents can open a Brimstone bakery. They can fill in for Albert while he's recovering. You can make it a family business. The tourist numbers would go through the roof. Everyone will race here, clamoring for a piece of pie from your parents. You must make that happen."

I shook my head. Nope. That was never happening. "Mom and Dad work hard all year. Maybe they want a break and to spend time with their family."

"Baking is in their blood. It's what they live for. Why would they not want to do that? You make the arrangements, and I'll set up the publicity. We can do a huge splash, front page spread, and multiple features on social media. It would attract national interest."

"Err... I'll speak to them and see what they have to say, but I'm promising nothing."

A cloud of glitter got dangerously close to my face. "You owe me."

"I don't owe you anything."

"The lies about the gem you've been pedaling have been giving me a headache."

I sighed. "If you can show me the gem right here and now, I'll believe in it and stop telling people it isn't real. Otherwise, my skepticism will remain in place."

"Some legends don't need proof. They simply are."

"That's ridiculous."

Rainbow huffed out a breath. "You need to get the bakery open. Find a way to do it. Don't let me down."

She wasn't giving up or going away, no matter how fast I walked. "I'll take a look at the store next door. Maybe we can set up something basic. But—"

"No buts. Get it done." She spun, glitter flying out around her, then shot into the sky and vanished.

I scurried past the discarded glitter, shaking my head. I hadn't missed baking for a second. It was nice not to mess up the desserts every day. And I didn't want to go through the hassle of setting up something temporary only for it to go wrong. I also didn't want to work with my parents. Rainbow would have to live without her treats, the same as everyone else.

There was a fork in the path, and I slowed. I'd been meaning to stop by and see Bart Hogarth to learn more about his arrangement with the treasure hunters.

I diverted away from the main path and took a curved route past a row of huge oak trees. The trees soon gave way to overgrown vegetable plots. Most of the plants had gone to seed, and what was left didn't look edible. It was all wrinkled and gray.

The white fence I walked up to was covered in faded white paint, and the gate was hanging by one hinge.

I couldn't remember the last time I'd been to Bart's house, and I'd never been inside, but everyone knew him. He kept himself to himself, preferring the company of the trees and the animals that lived in them to other magic users. He occasionally came into the village to get supplies and would often drop by the bakery. Uncle Albert was always happy to chat with him.

I walked past the gate and along an overgrown path to a sun-faded blue front door. I knocked on it.

A moment later, Bart opened it. He had a mess of white hair crowding around his head and huge white bushy eyebrows that shot up when he saw me. "Luna Brimstone! What brings you out here? I'm not selling any seedlings this year. I haven't had time to do any potting."

"Hi, Bart. I know my visit's unannounced, but I was just over with the gem hunters in the campsite. It's a bit of a mess over there, and I wanted to make sure you were doing okay. It must have shaken you up hearing about that poor man's murder."

He was silent for a second. "It did. You're not going after the gem too, are you?"

I smiled at him. "No. I'm supplying the food so they have plenty of fuel. Although I don't think they're planning on sticking around much longer."

His gaze lifted to the dark clouds. "I imagine not. Murder, rain storms, explosions. It's enough to put even the hardiest off."

"It is. How are you doing?"

Bart stepped out of the door, closing it behind him. "Not so bad. Don't mind if I don't invite you in. I rarely get guests, and the place isn't fit for such elegant company. We can take a walk around the fruit trees at the back if you like."

"Sure. That would be great. What are you growing this year?"

"Anything that doesn't die." Bart had a slight limp to his right leg as we took a slow walk away from the house. "I was sorry to hear what happened to Fandango's. How bad is it? I've not been into the village for weeks."

"It's gone. It was destroyed in the fire."

He shook his head. "That's a bad business. Your uncle was inside when it happened, wasn't he?"

"Yes. How did you know that?"

"I get my deliveries once a week. The boy dropping them off was full of the news. He couldn't stop talking about it."

"Uncle Albert was injured, but he should make a full recovery."

"I'm glad to hear it. I always enjoy shooting the breeze with your uncle." Bart sucked air through his teeth. "If I ever find that gem, I'll give you the money to help rebuild the place. I can't go without my special cakes for too long." He glanced at his house. "Of course, I need to fix this place up first. It's too big for me, but I enjoy the peace. And it's the only place I've ever lived. Moving so late in life would be too much of a hassle."

"That's generous of you to offer, but we've got insurance."

"Always sensible."

We walked side by side in silence for a moment.

"It's also good of you to let people look for the gem on your land. Doesn't it get annoying having strangers poking about?"

He ambled past a tired looking row of stunted apple trees. "It benefits all parties if they ever find it."

"What do you mean?" Torin had mentioned doing a deal with Bart, but I wanted to hear his side of the story.

"Some treasure hunters simply sneak into the woods and go looking. They don't last long. People who don't seek an invitation get ousted by the woodland creatures. And I give them a helping hand to see them on their way. Manners cost nothing. All they need to do is ask, and I'll happily let them on the land to poke around. But when they don't ask, I get unhappy."

"This latest group made sure it was okay to stay in the woods?"

"Yes, it was all official. And Killian is keeping an eye on things, getting them set up and making sure they don't pitch their tents on any rare flowers or disturb any nesting birds. They even agreed I could have a share of the gem when they found it." He shook his head and grinned. "They were convinced they'd find it and even showed me some information they'd put together. It was impressive. They were serious hunters."

"Did you think they had a chance of finding it?"

"Everyone thinks they're going to find the gem." His grin was sly. "It's one of the things that keeps me so busy. There's always some wide-eyed hopeful planning to unearth the gem and make their fortune."

I waggled my eyebrows. "Just between us, do you think it's real?"

His grin widened. "I'm hardly going to say it's not. It's one of the few sources of income I have left."

"People pay you to camp in the woods?"

"They do. But I charge fairly. The groups that don't know what they're doing get charged a basic rate. You sometimes get teenagers turning up wanting to snoop around for a few days. But this group, they were organized and had serious kit. They knew what they were doing and had a plan. So I charged them more. They didn't protest."

I slid him a glance. Bart always seemed friendly, but there was a motive for murder here. Did he think they'd gotten close to discovering the gem and had become greedy? The sad state of his orchard and house showed he was desperate for money, and the gem would have brought him untold riches.

He shook his head. "It's such a shame what happened to this group. I've never had anyone killed on my land before. There's been a few broken bones and bruises when inexperienced people got in over their heads but nothing like this."

"When did you first hear Alaric had been stabbed?"

"I got a visit from some sour-faced idiot from the Magic Council. I didn't like him. He had a smug look about him and kept peering at things that were no concern of his."

Bart had described Devlin perfectly. "Did he ask any questions?"

"He told me what was happening and that the site was being investigated. He asked if I'd heard anything unusual that night, but I'm a sound sleeper and am usually in bed early. I like to get up with the dawn. I feel more productive if I get things done early, rather than rolling around in bed and doing nothing. Plus, it doesn't help that I live alone. If I had a pretty wife to keep me company, I might be more inclined to not get up so early." He chuckled to himself.

I smiled as we continued a slow circle around the house. Bart seemed an unlikely suspect, and he wasn't fast moving or stealthy as he limped along. But he didn't have anyone to confirm his alibi, and that gem was a temptation. Perhaps he'd let his greed get the better of him.

He was going on my suspect list but right at the bottom. There were other people who'd had easier access to Alaric.

We completed the circuit of the house and stopped by his front door.

"Hopefully, you'll get less troublesome campers next time," I said. "I ran into Rainbow Dazzlewillow on my way here, and she was talking about making the most of this PR opportunity."

Bart grimaced. "She's always on at me to do more to promote the gem, but I chase her away with a broom. All she ever talks about is tourist numbers, profits, and maximizing opportunities. Sometimes, people just want to kick back and enjoy the breeze. What's wrong with that?"

I couldn't agree more. "Nothing that I can see. I'd better get going. I want to see how Uncle Albert is doing. He got out of the hospital last night."

"Give him my best. Tell him I already miss his apricot pastries with the white icing. Let me know when you're open again for business, and I'll be one of the first customers through the door. I'll make a special trip to the village to welcome you back."

"I will. Thanks for your time." I turned and headed along the path.

It was time to stop obsessing over this murder and enjoy some family time with my uncle.

Chapter 11

It had been a great afternoon, and I'd successfully avoided my parents for hours. They'd been out when I got back to Odessa's farmhouse, so I'd spent a blissful afternoon with only Uncle Albert.

He'd spent most of the time dozing in an easy chair by the window, a blanket tucked around him, while I sat opposite him, a book in one hand and a mug of hot chocolate in the other. Odessa had been working on the farm, and Earl was nowhere to be found.

Uncle Albert started in his chair, and his head jerked up.

I set down my book. "Hey. You've been asleep for ages. Good nap?"

He smacked his lips together and looked around. "Excellent. I needed it. After you left, your mom talked at me for about an hour."

"Eeek! Sorry to drop you in it like that, but I couldn't handle another interrogation."

"No apology needed. She's very persistent."

"They both are when they're trying to come out on top."

His forehead wrinkled as he looked at his bandaged hands.

"Time for a top up of healing salve?"

Uncle Albert nodded. "If you wouldn't mind. They aren't feeling comfortable."

"Let me grab the things from the bathroom." The hospital had sent us home with magic infused bandages and salve to speed up Uncle Albert's recovery.

Once I was settled in front of him, I carefully unwrapped his bandages and smoothed the healing salve over his hands, taking care not to cause any pain. "These are already looking better. It must be all the tender loving care Nurse Tabitha gave you."

His cheeks grew pink. "You could be right. I can't wait to bake again. It feels wrong not to have my hands in a mound of dough or be rolling out pastry cases for pie filling."

I hummed my agreement. I was loving not being in the bakery and messing up recipes. "Before I forget, Tabitha gave me her contact details so you can see each other once you're recovered. I think she's got a crush on you."

"Oh! Well.... I don't know what to say." He went beetroot red.

"If you like her too, I suggest you invite her for lunch or out for a walk when you're up to it. She seemed sweet. And you deserve sweet."

He bit his bottom lip. "I don't know. Would your auntie approve of this?"

"Of course! She'd want you to be happy and in love again. And you're not replacing her by dating.

You're just looking for a little joy. Wouldn't you like to see more of Tabitha?"

"Perhaps I could have her information, just in case."

I grinned at him. "I've left the paper with her number on it by your bed."

He nodded. "Perhaps we could come up with an afternoon tea menu to make for her. You must miss baking as much as me, so it would keep your mind occupied."

I unfurled the magic infused bandages and focused on those, not meeting his gaze. "Having a new routine is strange. As is having no place to call home."

"You could bake here. There's plenty of room, and I'm sure Odessa wouldn't mind. And you made the soup and sandwiches for the treasure hunting party, so you know where everything is."

"I wouldn't dare make anything complicated in case Mom and Dad saw what I was doing."

"They'd be thrilled to see you baking. They've mentioned a couple of times that you don't seem enthusiastic about being in the kitchen. Your dad's already insisted on making dinner."

"I'm amazed they've even noticed." I gently wrapped his first hand in a new bandage.

"Luna, they notice you. And while they get busy and caught up in their own worlds, they always want the best for you."

I sighed. "I know, but it feels weird having them around. Their previous visits have only been a day at the most. Have they said how long they're staying?"

"At least a week. Although your dad's been in contact with his current employer. I think he's already got itchy feet. Or probably itchy hands. Just like me, he wants to get back to the thing he loves."

I made another noncommittal noise as I wrapped his other hand. "How does that feel?"

"Like I'll be fine in a couple of weeks. I was so worried when I burned my hands. It makes me sick to think I might never bake again."

"You will. Before you know it, you'll be back in the amazing new Fandango's, and we'll have a queue of customers out the door begging for your food. I saw Bart Hogarth today, and he said he's already missing your treats."

"Did you see him in the woods?"

"Nope, I went to his house. I was asking a few questions about the treasure hunters. I thought he might know something."

"The Magic Council still hasn't figured out what happened to the poor fellow who was stabbed?"

"I'm sure they're working on it, but it never hurts to make sure they stay on track."

His eyebrows lowered. "Luna, do I need to remind you to be careful?"

"You don't. But it's important this murder is solved quickly. Mom and Dad are still worried Witch Haven is unsafe. I have to show them they have nothing to worry about. The quicker this murder gets solved, the better. Then they'll stop hassling me to leave."

"You really want to stay?"

I didn't miss the hint of hope in his voice. "Of course. We have a new bakery to get sorted."

"That could take a long time, though."

"Maybe not so long. I spoke to Rainbow Dazzlewillow today. She's keen on us finding a temporary solution so we can keep baking."

"What sort of solution?" His expression brightened.

"She's getting complaints about Fandango's not being open, so she suggested we run a temporary bakery from the store next door."

"The one used by the baking show? I didn't even think about that. I was thinking we wouldn't be able to do anything until our new store reopened. There's a kitchen in that old shop, isn't there?"

"Yes, but it's nothing like ours. They used to serve coffees and pastries you could heat up. It wouldn't be the same as Fandango's."

"We could invest in some basic equipment, though. Of course, we'll have to make sure it's up to standard so we can produce high-quality desserts. How exciting! We could have something running by the end of the month."

"We could, but don't get ahead of yourself. Your hands still need to heal before you bake anything."

"You run the place, and I'll be your silent baking partner. It could be a test run for you, for when the new Fandango's is open."

I stared at him, my stomach sinking. "You don't plan to run the new bakery?"

Uncle Albert shifted in his seat. "I'm thinking about taking a backseat. I'll still be around and will always want to bake, but when it opens, we could put your name above the door. It would attract new interest if it was being run by a Brimstone instead of a Black."

"People know the store is yours. They come for your food, not mine. Why change something that works so well?" And if I was in charge, it would turn into a giant, undercooked disaster. People would get food poisoning, we'd receive terrible ratings, and Fandango's would be ruined.

"Your parents have mentioned that I haven't pushed you enough, and perhaps your abilities have suffered." Uncle Albert dipped his chin. "I don't want to let you down."

My hand wrapped around my empty mug, and I gripped it. "Ignore them. They're saying that to convince you I should leave. They're guilt tripping you, and it's not fair."

"You would have more of a challenge if you were in charge of the bakery. You could oversee everything, from the menus to the opening hours. It would all be yours."

"I don't want that. Fandango's is yours. I'm not taking that from you because my parents are making veiled threats. I love working with you, and I want nothing to change."

"Things are changing, though. You've barely said anything about your surprise wedding announcement." His gaze was full of questions.

"I'm not hiding it, but like you said, it was a surprise for everyone. I'm getting used to the idea I could marry Cole."

"Only could? You're not certain about him?"

Settling back on my heels, I considered my next words carefully. "I'm adjusting to the idea."

"Luna, if you're not committed to him, you don't have to rush anything. Your parents are thrilled you're marrying into such an esteemed werewolf family, but don't make hasty decisions because of that."

"I had no clue Cole came from such an impressive family. And I wouldn't care if he had no connections. I like him. He's a decent guy, and he's been great to me. The short time we've known each other, we've had rocky patches, but he's been steadfast. I love that about him."

Uncle Albert nodded. "I can see he makes you happy. Whenever he's around, you're always smiling. That's good. But make sure you take time to get to know each other. How many dates have you been on?"

I blushed. "We had our first official date the day the bakery caught fire. But I've known him longer than that." Although it wasn't that long. Was I being an idiot for rushing into this marriage?

Uncle Albert gently rested a bandaged hand on top of mine. "The heart knows when it's found the right one. I hadn't been on a single date with your auntie, and I was head over heels in love with her. She was so beautiful and vibrant, and her pastries were intoxicatingly tasty. She always lit up the room when she walked in, and she was kind to everyone. I had a crush on her for years before making a move, and she probably didn't even know my name."

I loved it when he spoke about my auntie. We all missed her. "That's not true. She liked you just as much, but you were both too shy to say anything to each other."

"We should never have waited. We missed opportunities because we were so hesitant." He nodded. "I'm happy you're not doing that with Cole. He is devoted to you. Forget my cautions. It's just an old man worrying about his favorite niece. If you love him and he makes you happy, then you have my full blessing."

"Thanks. That means a lot. And I am happy with Cole." I fell silent. I wasn't faking my feelings about Cole. This was what I wanted, and it felt great to have something concrete and sure. With the bakery gone, my parents hassling me to make changes, and my unstable magic, having one certain thing in my life was what I needed.

Earl strolled into the kitchen. "Your parents are back."

I watched him strut across the floor. "We're talking now?"

"When were we ever not talking?" He sat facing the window, not looking at me.

I didn't want to argue with Earl in front of Uncle Albert, so I scooped him up and settled him on my shoulder. "Let's head to Fandango's. We can take a look at the store next door and see if it's suitable for setting up a temporary bakery."

"You want me to come with you?" Earl shifted about on my shoulder as if he was considering jumping off.

"Why not?" And it would beat an interrogation from my parents the second they saw me. "Uncle Albert, are you okay if we go?"

"Of course. Go see about that empty store. It could be just what we need." He glanced out the window. "And don't worry, I'll fend off your parents. I'll say you're busy on bakery business. That'll keep them happy."

I kissed his cheek. "Thanks. I'll see you later." I snuck out the back door before my parents caught me.

Earl curled around my shoulders, although he wasn't relaxed.

I slid around the side of the house and waited until I could no longer hear my parents' voices before hurrying away.

"Still keeping secrets?"

I glanced at Earl. "I'm not sure I follow."

"Hiding from your parents. Why is that? What don't you want them to know?"

"You know why I'm skipping out on them. They expect too much from me, and they always take over." I dashed past rows of large, looming scarecrows, making sure not to make eye contact.

"Maybe leaving Witch Haven wouldn't be so bad."

"Not for you. And I thought you were already making other plans. The last time we talked, you were putting up ads to find a new witch."

"I'm still thinking about that. I need a purpose."

"Have you been on a bad batch of catnip? Is that what's making you so grouchy?"

"I'm off the catnip."

I slowed my pace. "Since when?"

"Since the fire. I was thinking... maybe I could have done more to help. I could have stopped Albert from getting injured."

"Earl! There was nothing you could have done."

He was quiet. "I heard something."

"The night of the fire?"

"Yes. I was... intoxicated with catnip. I was annoyed about the dog, so I needed some light relief."

"What dog?"

"The one you're marrying without asking my permission."

"Cole's not a dog. And he's going to be my husband, so be nice to him." I grinned. "Husband! How weird is that?"

"No weirder than you not bothering to tell your familiar there'd be a pack beast living with me."

"I didn't think you had a problem with werewolves."

"I'm a cat!"

"Uh, okay. I should have checked. But Cole has great control of his wolf. Besides, we weren't speaking." It looked like I'd just found someone else who was annoyed with me for not shouting about my engagement to the world. I should make a list of those I'd wronged. It would be long. "Go back to the night of the fire. You said you heard a noise?"

"I think so. But I'd snuffed up a lot of catnip. My ears were ringing, and I kept seeing things that weren't there. If I hadn't been so cat-nipped out, I might have investigated the sound. It could have been the arsonist setting his explosive magic."

"If you had investigated, whoever it was might have killed you."

"Doubtful. I'm tough." He relaxed a fraction. "Do you have any idea who hates Fandango's enough to torch it with us inside?"

"Yes."

"And what are you going to do about it?"

"Stop him from ever doing it again." I had no plan how to find Bram Vexx, but I would, and I'd make him sorry.

"From what your parents keep saying, you won't be around for much longer, anyway. You won't care about Fandango's once you're gone."

"That's not true. That's their plan for me. I have other ideas."

"If ever you want to let me in on those plans, I might be around to listen."

"Oh, don't be like that. I know things haven't been great between us, but I want us both to be happy."

"We know the solution to finding that happiness, don't we?"

"We do?"

"Stop hiding the fact you hate baking."

"I don't hate it."

"Yes, you do. The same as me. We want more from life than apple strudel and pumpkin pie. We need excitement and danger and—"

"Since when have either of us wanted that? I crave a quiet life. And you only care about catnip."

"Not if the energy crackling out of you is anything to go by. It affects me the same as it does you. Our familiar bond is weak, but it's still there. You force your magic to do something that feels unnatural, so of course, it breaks when you use it."

A huff of frustration shot out of me. "If I'm not meant to bake, what should I do?"

"Find a solution before you ruin this for good."

"This meaning us?"

"This meaning everything you care about. Including the werewolf and your family. And me."

I stomped along, not knowing what to do with the exasperation pounding in my chest. "Let's not discuss this. There's too much else going on. I need to focus on one thing at a time. Having a tetchy familiar who thinks he's something he's not isn't helping. Let's go see the store next to the bakery and figure out if that will make Uncle Albert happy. I don't want him missing out on what he loves to do."

"What about what you love?" Earl muttered.

I gritted my teeth. "If I knew the answer to that, I'd be doing it."

We walked the rest of the way in a tense silence.

My heart ached that Earl was so unhappy with me, but I didn't have a solution. I knew what my magic was supposed to do, and it was hardly my fault it didn't behave the way it should. Besides, I hadn't insisted Earl get stuck with me.

Since we were such a bad fit, maybe it was better if we went our separate ways. Earl could find a witch better suited to him, and I'd go without or invest in a new familiar. Many magic users got by without them.

Tears filled my eyes, but I blinked until they were gone. I'd miss having this little fuzz ball around if he left me.

Earl tensed at the same time as me. "Did you hear shouting?"

I looked around as we walked along the street. "It's two guys, but I don't see them." I rounded the corner and stopped. Torin stood in front of

Devlin. He was yelling in his face and jabbing a finger against his chest.

Killian was also there, standing by his truck, alarm written all over his face.

"I demand you give me protection," Torin yelled. "There has already been two attempts on my life. The next one could succeed. It's your job to make sure that doesn't happen."

"You need to calm down." Devlin took a step back, the color high in his cheeks. "We don't know for certain anyone is trying to kill you."

"It's not a person. It's the gem. It wants me dead. It has me in its sights. What if it doesn't stop?" Torin yanked at his hair. "I need you to give me around-the-clock protection."

Devlin shook his head. "We don't have the budget for that."

Torin roared and swung a wild punch. It slammed into Devlin's nose.

He yelped and stumbled back, his hands going to his nose.

Killian raced over and grabbed Torin, stopping him before he launched another punch.

I hurried over to the fight with Earl still on my shoulders, although he was now sitting parrot fashion and his whiskers were twitching.

"Don't! You're only making this worse for yourself if you hit him again," Killian said.

"He has to offer me protection," Torin said. "The man's incompetent. People are dying, and he's doing nothing. All he cares about is his budget."

"I get that you're scared, but don't punch members of the Magic Council." Killian tugged Torin back a few steps.

"Is everything okay?" I said as I reached them.

Torin wrenched himself out of Killian's grip and turned on me. He heaved out a sigh. "Oh, it's you. I'm trying to get the Magic Council to help me. Maybe you can talk sense into this moron. Tell him what happened at our camp."

I doubted I'd be much good at convincing Devlin to do anything, given my tangled history with him. Still, I wanted to help. "Devlin, Torin has a point. Something weird is going on."

He didn't even look at me. "You're under arrest for assault." Devlin sounded muffled as he continued to grip his nose.

"You're putting me behind bars?" Torin said.

"There's no need for that," I said. "Torin's just upset. One of his friends was killed, and he was almost hit by a boulder."

"That's exactly what I'm doing." Devlin was still pretending I wasn't there. Perhaps he hoped if he ignored me for long enough, I'd go away.

Torin threw up his hands. "Finally! If I'm locked up, at least I'm safe."

Devlin blinked several times, as if not expecting that response. "Come with me."

"So long as you put me somewhere this curse can't get me, I'll happily follow you."

Devlin grabbed Torin's elbow and headed to Olympus's office at the end of the street.

Killian blew out a breath as we followed along behind them. "I'm worried about Torin. He's not been himself since Alaric got stabbed."

"That's hardly a surprise, especially since he's convinced he's next on the list."

He dragged a hand through his tousled hair. "I feel terrible about taking them to the campsite. I never expected this to happen. The other groups I've helped always thought it was just a game. They'd look around for a bit and then leave when the novelty wore off or it got cold."

"Do you think this group of treasure hunters got close to the gem?"

"I'm not even sure it's real. This was just a way for me to make some money." He glanced back at his truck. "I can't stay. I'm transporting a long-tailed slink rat to the refuge. I only pulled over because I saw Torin arguing with Devlin and wanted to see what was going on."

I looked back at the truck and saw a timid furry face with big eyes peering from out of the window. "You go. I'll keep an eye on Torin and see what's happening."

"Thanks. Maybe I need to rethink taking people into the woods if they're going to behave like this. Fun should never be dangerous." Killian turned and hurried back to his truck.

"What do you reckon the odds are Devlin will throw us out if we go to the office and ask about Torin?" I said to Earl.

"There's only one way to find out."

I drew in a deep breath and headed to Olympus's office. I opened the door without knocking.

Monty, Olympus's familiar, bounded over, his tail swishing and his eyes bright with excitement. "You just missed a fight. It was so exciting. I tried to help, but Devlin said I was a nuisance. I'm not a nuisance, am I?"

I petted his huge head. "You're never a nuisance. What's going on?"

"Devlin's eyes are watering. He's crying about something. Olympus went through the back to process that guy who smells of the woods. He's locking him up."

"Did Torin change his mind about going in a cell? He fought Devlin to get away?"

"No! Devlin said he'd let him off with a warning because he was upset, so Torin thumped him straight in the face. Then he got dragged away by Olympus. Devlin's lip was bleeding." Monty looked at Earl. "Hey! Have you got any of that catnip? It's great stuff."

"I'm almost out. But I'm not using it anymore." Earl's claws dug into my shoulder.

I perched on the edge of the seat and waited for, hopefully, Olympus to return from the cells.

"That catnip was fun, although it gave me a headache the next day, and all I wanted to do was eat and sleep. Olympus kept saying I was the laziest creature he'd ever met." Monty sniffed me. "You smell like a rainforest!"

"Um... thanks. I'm using a new shampoo."

"Catnip can do that to you if you're not used to it." Earl hopped off my shoulders and settled on a visitor's chair. "I'm thinking of taking up yoga instead."

I couldn't help the laugh that blurted out of me. "Yoga! I can't imagine you doing that."

"And I can't imagine you making the perfect soufflé, yet you still insist on trying."

I huffed out a breath. "I will one day."

Stomping footsteps drawing near had me looking up. Devlin marched into the office. He was still holding his nose. "It's broken! I'm charging him with assault. Look at my face."

Olympus was close behind him, his expression grim. "Torin is terrified. He thinks someone's going to kill him. Cut him some slack."

"It's not your nose he broke." Devlin glared at me. "What are you doing here?"

Olympus stood between us. "I asked Luna to come over to go through the paperwork about the bakery fire."

My eyebrows shot up, but I nodded. "That's right."

Olympus grinned at me and winked without Devlin seeing. "We won't be a moment. We're just tidying up a problem."

"Don't let Torin out of that cell," Devlin said. "He's dangerous."

"Only when he's being provoked by you," I muttered.

Olympus looked like he was trying not to laugh. "I'll keep Torin here for now. But he's your arrest, so you deal with the paperwork."

"I will. But I need to get my nose seen by a doctor. I'll be back." Devlin shot me one more glare and left the office.

Olympus sighed and sank into his seat. "There are some days, when I also want to punch Devlin Goody in the nose. The guy is so uptight."

"I remember someone else who used to be like that."

He arched an eyebrow. "Let's not go there. I've learned my lesson. Work isn't everything."

"Thanks for covering for me. I didn't mean to get involved, but I saw the fight between Devlin and Torin and wanted to make sure Torin was okay."

"He'll be fine in the cell. But he's panicked. He genuinely thinks he's the next target for this gem curse. Do you know anything about that?"

"A bit. I've been going to the campsite most days and taking their food. At first, I don't think they believed in it, but then Alaric was stabbed, and Torin almost got splatted by a flying boulder..."

He nodded. "Indigo was telling me last night what's been going on over there. I always thought that gem was a myth."

"I still think it is. I hope it is. Otherwise, we have seriously dangerous magic lurking in our woods." I glanced at the closed door leading to the cell. "Is there any chance I can see Torin?"

"It's best you don't. He needs time to cool down. And so does Devlin. I don't think his nose is broken, but he'll have a bruise and a fat lip. And he won't let Torin get away with this."

The main office door opened, and Mitchell Collery strode through.

"Hi, Mitchell. Perfect timing," Olympus said.

I nodded at him. "I've been meaning to visit you."

"That's why I'm here, isn't it?" Mitchell was a man mountain, with wide shoulders and a neat dark beard framing a friendly face with lots of smile lines.

"Oh! I didn't realize this was an official meeting." I glanced at Olympus. "You were telling the truth about going over the bakery report?"

"In a way. I'd planned to meet Mitchell to go over the case file," Olympus said. "You're welcome to join us. You could find it useful. I was going to get in touch later and give you a summary of our findings since there's a lot to go through."

"I'd like to know everything. I'm happy to stay, if that's okay."

Mitchell settled in a chair. "It's fine by me. But I warn you, these reports are long, and it gets boring if you're not into building schematics, fire patterns, salvage activities, and weather conditions, among other things."

"Sounds good. I want to hear it all."

"I'll make some coffee," Olympus said.

Three hours later, and I was struggling not to doze. Neither of them had exaggerated when they'd said the report was detailed. Mitchell had gone over every element of the investigation. Some of it was interesting, but a lot had gone over my head. Fire suppression activities, personnel movements, external source contamination, and so on. I was grateful he was being thorough, but it wasn't all that fascinating.

Mitchell stretched his arms over his head and then settled his large hands on his knees. "Luna, you need to know, Devlin Goody added some notes to the file. I have questions to ask you. Do you have any objections if I ask them now? It doesn't need to be official."

"Go ahead. I want this sorted as soon as possible. I'll help in any way I can."

"That's good of you." Mitchell nodded slowly as he pursed his lips. "Devlin thinks you have money worries."

My spine stiffened, and my jaw clenched. So, it was those kinds of questions. Trust Devlin to suspect me. "That's not true. The bakery is a successful business."

"Devlin's not so interested in the bakery finances, but your personal finances. And he suggested you've been failing to do your job properly."

My hands flexed into fists. "I always do my job to the best of my ability. You should know, Devlin Goody has a personal grudge against me. He's been hassling me about my magic for ages. I can't figure out why he doesn't like me, but he just doesn't. He even tried to charge me with a murder I had nothing to do with. Ever since then, he's been on my back."

"You shouldn't pay too much attention to Devlin's comments in the file," Olympus said. "He gets the bit in between his teeth and won't let go. Luna's an honest, decent witch."

"I don't disagree with any of that, but I have to ask these questions," Mitchell said. "Devlin is concerned you started the fire because you wanted the insurance payout before he closed down Fandango's."

"He was going to close Fandango's?" I lurched forward in my seat. "He's made threats to do such a thing, but I didn't think he was serious."

"Devlin details his concerns about your magic and argues you were serving unsafe food. He has evidence to support his claims."

I pressed my lips together, a headache pounding behind my eyes. "You've eaten at Fandango's plenty of times. Did you ever have any ill effects?"

Mitchell smiled. "Never. And as soon as it's rebuilt, I'm coming right back. But Devlin is a respected member of the Magic Council, and he's in a position of authority. His concerns need to be followed up. And the fire was arson. As you saw from the report, there were three concentrated blasts of magic in the bakery."

"I didn't do that."

"I'm not saying you did. And I believe Devlin is just setting out all possibilities. He's always been thorough in his work."

"There's another way to describe that, but I'm not cursing," I said. "I wasn't even in the bakery. He's wrong about this. Same as always."

Mitchell's eyebrows rose at my sharp tone. "Do you have any idea who might have set those magic blasts?"

I wasn't mentioning Bram. I was dealing with him. "No one springs to mind. Apart from Devlin, everyone loves the place."

"I'll speak to Devlin about this," Olympus said. "Luna, you have nothing to worry about. I know you'd never hurt your family."

"That's right." I looked at Earl, who was snoozing on the chair.

"Then I think we're done here," Mitchell said. "I'll leave Devlin to follow up on his questions if he needs more information. And you have a solid alibi. There's no way you could have started that fire."

"Thanks. I appreciate that," I said.

Mitchell said his goodbyes, collected his paperwork, and left the office.

After he'd gone, I let out a sigh. "That was intense."

"Mitchell always is. But he's excellent at his job. He doesn't miss a thing."

"You don't think there'll be any trouble getting the insurance payout because of Devlin's concerns about me, do you?"

"I shouldn't think so. And I'll back you up on this." Olympus checked the time. "But it would be good if we could find out who did it."

"We will. I'm sure of that."

Olympus tilted his head. "Is there anything you want to share?"

My gaze flicked away from him for a second. "No, I don't know anything."

He nodded, but his eyes were narrowed, suggesting he didn't believe me. "I need to check on Torin. Hopefully, he's calmer now and less likely to swing punches in my direction."

I sat back in my seat and picked up my mug, frowning when I realized it was empty.

Devlin walked back into the office, a butterfly stitch on his lower lip. "Oh! You're still here."

"I'm happy to see you, too." I slammed down my mug. "We had a lot to talk about. Including the fact you pointed the finger at me for the fire. Why do you hate me so much?"

His hand went to his dull red nose. "I don't hate you. I'm just doing my job."

There was a yell, and Olympus raced back into the office. "Torin's dead!"

Chapter 12

No one moved for a few seconds as the shock of Olympus's words hit.

"What do you mean, he's dead?" Devlin strode past Olympus and into the cell. "Are you sure he's not asleep?"

I raced after them, Monty right beside me. My hand flew to my mouth as I took in the scene inside the cell. There was no mistake. Torin lay flat on his back, his sightless eyes staring at the ceiling. His skin was gray, and his tongue poked out from between swollen lips.

"How is this possible?" Devlin's voice shook. "He was inside a locked cell. Who got to him? Did he have any visitors while I was gone?"

Olympus glanced at me, shock registering on his face. "We've been here this whole time. No one came into the office other than Mitchell. There's no way anyone got to this cell without us noticing."

Devlin stepped through the open cell door and knelt beside Torin. He checked his pulse. "He's already going cold. This must have happened almost as soon as we put him in here."

"Could it be an allergic reaction to something? Look how he's all swollen up," I said.

Devlin didn't look at me. "That's not possible. There's nothing in here for him to be allergic to."

Olympus shook his head. "We didn't give Torin anything to eat or drink. And the cell is bare."

Devlin stood and stepped back. His face was pale and his shoulders tight. "Was it something I did? I was rough when I arrested him. I was angry because he punched me. And when he punched me again, I shoved him away. Did I do this?"

"No! I saw how you handled Torin outside," I said. "You weren't that rough with him. And you had to protect yourself."

He glanced at me. "You'll testify to that?"

"Sure, if it comes to it. But you didn't do this to Torin."

Olympus nodded. "This has nothing to do with you, Devlin. We both restrained him after he assaulted you. We followed the right procedures."

My gaze went around the cell. There had to be something in here that got to Torin and made him bloat up like an ugly gray beach ball.

Nobody liked looking at a dead body, but as Devlin and Olympus talked, I forced myself to study Torin. His eyes were bulging, and there was a strange gray tint covering the skin I could see. He was horribly swollen with puffy lips and eyelids. Even his fingers looked bloated.

"Maybe Torin had something on him that did this," I said. "Did he have food in his pockets?"

Devlin turned slowly and his eyes widened. "I... I didn't do a thorough enough search. I patted him down, but I must have missed something. I just wanted him locked up and out of my way. This is my fault."

Olympus frowned. "The magic around the cell didn't detect anything odd. And why would Torin have something on him that had the potential to kill him? That makes no sense."

"There'll be an investigation. This looks bad. I could lose my promotion," Devlin said. "And I've worked so hard. They can't take it away from me."

Olympus made a disgusted sound in the back of his throat. "Stop panicking about your job."

"Of course I'm panicking. This is my career on the line. And potentially yours. You're involved too," Devlin said. "I'm not in this alone."

The initial trickle of sympathy I felt for Devlin vanished. Of course, he'd try to drag Olympus down with him if there was any trouble. "This isn't Olympus's fault. You arrested Torin. You should have made sure he was safe before locking him in the cell."

"I thought he was." Devlin's shoulders sank.

Olympus glanced at me and shook his head. "We need to leave this scene untouched. We'll get a team in to examine everything. There could be something we've missed."

"I should go to the Magic Council and tell them what I've done," Devlin said. "If I get ahead of this, I might keep my job."

"No one is losing their job. We'll figure out what happened. There'll be an explanation."

I backed away as Olympus and Devlin moved out of the cell and shut the door.

"Devlin, go grab the forms we need from the store room to record this incident," Olympus said. "I'll contact a team to run a sweep."

Devlin turned and walked away, his knees looking like they might give out on him at any second.

"What am I going to do with that idiot?" Olympus said. "I know there's a good person hiding in there, but Devlin makes it so hard on himself."

"I kind of feel sorry for him, even though he was a jerk to you."

"Sometimes, he takes the letter of the law too literally. But then he misses things like this." Olympus raised a finger. "And before you say it, I know I used to be like that. But was I really so terrible to be around?"

"Kind of. Until Indigo loosened you up, you sort of sucked."

"Thanks." His gaze cut to Torin's body, and he sighed. "This is a mess."

"It calls for more coffee," I said.

"I'll make it. You go back to the office. You don't want to be in here with the body."

I was happy to follow Olympus, but I slowed when I spotted a small green dot of liquid on the floor. I looked around but couldn't see any more.

Then I took a few more steps and found another one. The green dots led me back to the main office.

When I got in there, Earl was growling, and he was off the seat. His fur was puffed up, and he had his back to me, facing the corner of the room.

"Hey! What are you doing?"

He didn't respond to my question, simply hissed and lowered his ears.

"I told him not to touch it." Monty's voice came from underneath Olympus's desk.

"Touch what? Is there a mouse?" I walked over to Earl and peered over his shoulder. There was a tiny purple frog with black dots on it. It was backed right against the wall, its eyes unblinking.

Earl hissed again and swiped at the frog. "Stay back. It's poisonous."

"Are you sure? It's so small."

"It's small but deadly." Monty must have been shaking, because the desk was wobbling. "It's a purple devil frog. The worst kind. They're so mean. All they enjoy doing is killing."

My jaw dropped. "I've heard of them. They're rare, and their venom can kill a Big Foot."

"Hide!" Monty hissed. "It's angry. It tried to get me, and I was being nice to it."

I took a step back just as the frog leaped. I squeaked and stumbled away, shielding my face from any venom.

Earl flipped into the air, grabbed the frog in his mouth, and bit down.

There was a huge popping noise, and pain blazed through my body as I collapsed to the floor.

***

Ever so slowly, I opened my eyes. I had no idea where I was. The last thing I remembered was being hit by a bone jarring pain in Olympus's office. It had flared through my body like a wildfire, sizzling my blood and shaking my spine.

This wasn't his office. The ceiling and walls were white, and there was a faint smell of something antiseptic.

"Hey, you're awake." Cole's blurry face came into view, and I felt his hand wrap around mine.

"Where am I?" I croaked out.

"You're in the hospital." My mom appeared on the other side of the bed, alongside my dad. They wore matching masks of concern.

"How did I get here?" My body still throbbed with pain, like I was one giant bruise. What had happened to me?

"Olympus brought you in." Indigo appeared at the end of the bed, and alongside her were Storm and Odessa.

"You're all here?"

"Me included." Uncle Albert showed his face. "Even though your parents said I should be resting, there was no way I was leaving you. Not after what happened."

I shook my head, too groggy to make sense of all of this. "I don't know what happened. Can someone fill me in?"

No one spoke as looks passed among the group.

"You don't remember?" Cole said.

"Some of it. I was in Olympus's office, and we'd just spent an eternity going over the report on the bakery fire. And then... Torin got arrested for punching Devlin on the nose. No, that happened before the fire report meeting. Torin got arrested and put in a cell, and then we went through the report. We found him dead after that. Devlin was panicking and trying to figure out what to do."

"That's right," my mom said.

I shook my head gingerly, pain burning behind my eyes. "There was a... frog? Am I remembering right? It all happened so fast. The frog jumped at me."

Cole squeezed my hand. "Olympus didn't see it happen, but he thinks you discovered the creature that killed Torin. It was a purple devil frog."

"I thought I'd dreamt that. There really was a frog. What was it doing in his office?"

"They're still figuring that out," Indigo said. "The Magic Council is investigating the site. It shouldn't have been there. They're not sure if it was planted as an attack on the Magic Council or Torin."

"I saw green spots on the floor, and they led me to the frog. Oh! And Earl. How's he doing? He bit the frog. He stopped it from getting me. He grabbed it, and then I got slammed with this pain. I feel gross."

"Oh, sweetheart. I'm so sorry. We thought you'd already sense what happened to him," my mom said.

"I'm struggling here. I can't fit all the pieces together. What am I supposed to know about Earl?"

Mom gripped my free hand. "You don't sense it?"

"Please, just tell me. I must have passed out."

"For two days," Cole said. "You've been in the hospital for forty-eight hours."

I gulped. "It was that bad?"

Dad patted my knee under the covers. "When a witch's familiar dies, it always injures the witch they're bonded to."

I stared at him and closed my eyes for a second. I couldn't have heard that right. "Earl is dead?"

"It's why you feel so bad. Earl stopped that poisonous frog from touching you. It would have killed you just as it did Torin. Earl's a hero," Indigo said.

A sharp pain lanced through my heart, but I still couldn't believe it. "He protected me?"

"Earl saved your life. He could see what a threat that frog was and was determined not to let it hurt you," my mom said.

"But... he's not dead." Tiny pieces of my shattered heart crumbled away. I'd always underestimated Earl. I'd ignored him, treated him more like a normal cat than a witch's familiar, and never taken him seriously. No wonder he'd turned to catnip to distract himself. He must have been bored out of his mind being saddled with a malfunctioning witch.

"We'll do something special to remember him when you're strong enough." Odessa wiped her eyes. "He was such a sweetie. We'll make sure Earl is never forgotten."

I wanted to pull the covers over my head and vanish. All the sympathy and sad looks coming my way were too intense. I cleared my throat. "I need to see him."

"It's not a good idea," my mom said. "You'll only upset yourself. And you need to rest. Without your familiar, it'll take a while for you to heal."

"I won't believe it until I see him for myself."

"We figured you'd say that," Storm said. "The Magic Council tried to take him away. They said he was evidence."

"You didn't let them, did you?"

Storm smirked. "Of course not. I kept him for you in a stasis spell. Shall I go get him?"

"Yes. And I want to be alone with him."

"You shouldn't be on your own," my mom said. "I'll stay with you."

I looked around the group, their images blurry from the tears I held back. "Please, I have to be with my familiar. I need to say a proper goodbye to him."

More troubling glances were exchanged, then Cole stood. He squeezed my hand and turned to everyone. "You heard Luna. She wants to be on her own. Everyone clear the room."

My mom opened her mouth as if she was about to protest, but my dad caught hold of her elbow. "Let's give Luna some space. We'll be right outside when you need us." He gently tugged Mom away from the bed.

They'd just reached the door when the room darkened.

I blinked, and it took me a few seconds to realize water was hitting my face. I looked at the ceiling, expecting to see a leak, but it was raining inside the room. "What's going on?"

Odessa and Indigo stood either side of my bed, determined looks on their faces. "We'll fix this. Everyone else out."

The rain increased, and large, fat blobs of snow swirled in the mix.

Mom stared at me for a second, her cheeks blanched of color and a touch of what looked like horror in her eyes.

I gestured for her to leave. "Go with Dad. And take Uncle Albert with you. We'll get this under control."

Although I had no clue how, I just needed to be on my own.

After a few seconds of hesitation, she nodded, gathered up Uncle Albert, and they left the room.

Cole kissed my damp cheek. "Let me know if there's anything I can do to make you feel better." He rested his forehead against mine.

I moved my lips to his ear. "Go to my farmhouse. I haven't been there for days, and they'll be worried. You know how to break through the magic."

His worried gaze met mine. "I don't want to leave you."

"I have plenty of people looking out for me. I won't settle until I know they're okay."

He kissed me again. "Of course. But I won't be long." He dashed from the room.

I looked at Odessa and Indigo. Neither of them were moving. "You can go, too."

Indigo's lips were pressed together. "That's not happening."

The door opened, and Storm came in with a small bundle in her arms. Her gaze cut to the fat snowflakes and rain, and she sighed. "I figured this would happen. I'm surprised it took so long."

My chest tightened as I stared at the blanket in her arms, not fully registering her words. "Is that..."

She nodded and placed the bundle on the bed.

It was almost impossible for me to swallow as my tears mingled with the snow and rain. This couldn't be Earl. It was too small. "You can all go."

"No. We stay." Indigo held her hands out to the others, and they connected and surrounded the bed. "Storm, can you do something about this weather?"

"I've nudged it, but it's powerful. It doesn't want to leave. Luna doesn't want it to go."

"I don't care why it's happening. And it's a perfect match for my mood," I whispered. "It can stick around if it wants to."

"If that's what you'd prefer, then it stays," Storm said. "After all, your magic is doing this."

"No, it's not!" I stared at my friends.

They all met my gaze, none of them wavering or judging, just waiting.

A shaky breath came out of my lips. I was exhausted, broken, and my familiar was gone. My magic didn't work, and now my oldest friends thought I was making it snow in my hospital room.

Indigo, Odessa, and Storm simply waited, their gentle friendship magic sliding over me and lessening the pain around my heart.

I drew in a shuddering breath as snow swirled around the room and the rain soaked us. "My magic has never worked how I wanted it to. I've tried everything to fix it, but nothing holds for long."

"What kind of things have you tried?" Indigo said.

"Enhancement potions, meditation, relaxation techniques, healing crystals, but none of them had an effect. That's when I tried other methods and got in trouble."

"The Bram Vexx kind of trouble," Storm said.

I closed my eyes for a few seconds. "Yes. I never meant to get in over my head, but Uncle Albert needed me, and I couldn't let him down. I had to step up and take on more responsibility at the bakery, but my magic wasn't up to it. So... I paid for a few magic boosts through Bram. He put me in touch with a magic lender."

"You borrowed magic?" Odessa said.

"It was only meant to be a couple of times, but before I knew it, I needed more and more. Then I didn't have enough money to pay for it all, so I got it on credit. I always meant to pay it back."

"You accepted credit from someone as shady as Bram?" Storm said.

I nodded. "From his boss. Bram's the muscle. How did you find out who he really is?"

"I checked his background. He's not a nice guy."

"Neither is the guy he works for. But I was desperate. And... there's something else." I pressed my lips together, almost too scared to reveal everything. "I have a small harem of magic users who live in a farmhouse I keep hidden from people."

Odessa's eyes widened. "What do you use them for?"

"Not what you think. They needed help, so I offered them a safe place. They let me drain their magic to keep mine stable. It was a great set up, until it stopped working and I had to rely on other sources just to get by." I gulped back tears. "I didn't mean to keep this from you, but I didn't want to let anyone down."

Indigo sighed. "Other than yourself, you haven't let anyone down. But you've been so busy pretending everything was fine that you messed up your own life."

"Everything was fine. I was managing in the bakery, and my little group of magic users were content. No one knew I had a problem."

"But it wasn't working," Storm said. "And your magic has always been different. We've always known that." Her gaze slid to the small pile of snow on the end of my bed.

"You... have?" They couldn't know what a screw-up I really was.

"Of course we have," Odessa said. "We were always offering to help you, but you never wanted it."

"You always said you were fine." Storm's top lip curled. "You're a terrible liar."

"I just wanted a quiet life and not to worry people. Now everything's broken. The bakery is gone, and I don't know what's going on with my magic." I gestured at the snow. "And Earl's dead. I never took him seriously. I let him down, and now I've lost him."

Odessa flipped wet hair out of her eyes. "This weather magic feels powerful, but you need to control it before we all get frozen toes."

"I don't know how! Is this even me? That's why I'm in this mess. I've never known how to control magic. When I use spells in my baking, which they're supposed to be perfect for, they don't do what they should."

"We've eaten enough of your cookies to know that's the truth," Indigo said.

"This isn't baking magic," Storm said. "And your magic has always felt strange to me, but now I know why. You've been using other people's magic. But when you use your own power, you feel more like me. The power surrounding us is elemental magic."

"That's impossible. My parents are natural bakers. I can't be anything else."

"You are. And you need to get used to that. You also need to learn to control it, before this whole place goes underwater, or we get buried in a snowdrift," Storm said.

"It's not me doing this." I pinched the bridge of my nose. "It can't be."

"It's not any of us," Indigo said. "And this freaky indoor weather started when you learned about Earl."

I shook my head. They were making a mistake. And when they took the time to process what I'd told them, they'd judge me. I'd lied to them for years, and they wouldn't want a failed witch as a friend.

"I want to be on my own. I have to say goodbye to Earl."

"We don't want to leave you," Odessa said, "not when you're so sad. Your heartache is making it snow."

"Just go!" A blast of icy wind shot around the room and slammed into my friends.

Storm took a step back. "Luna! This magic is your doing. You need to accept that. You'll never control this power until you embrace it."

"Don't shove us away. We'll do whatever it takes to figure out why you don't have baking magic," Indigo said.

"I'm not. But I can't handle this right now. I have to focus on Earl. He's all I care about." My throat hurt from holding back all the tears that wanted to choke out of me.

I looked at Earl. The blanket covering him was drenched, along with everything else in the room. I stared at him, not able to look my friends in the eyes. I was so ashamed. This was the end of everything I'd built up. It had all fallen apart around me.

"Give me ten minutes," I whispered.

"You don't have to do this alone," Indigo said. "But sure, take a few minutes. We'll be outside when you need us."

I kept my eyes closed until I heard the door shut, then I gathered Earl against my chest and held him close. Icy shards dug into my freezing skin as Storm's stasis magic pulsed gently around Earl.

The blanket was heavy as I eased it back so I could see his furry face. He looked peaceful with his eyes closed. I hoped he hadn't suffered saving my worthless butt from that poisonous frog.

My tears fell harder as the rain beat down. "I'm so sorry for everything. For hiding things from you, not taking you seriously, and thinking you were useless."

Snow pelted against my face, and I could barely breathe.

"I never thought I was a good enough witch to have you. You could have done so much better than me. You'd have been happy with someone else, and you could have used your magic to have a great life. Instead, you got stuck with me." I ran my hands over his body. Magic was pulsing out of me in waves I had no control over.

The snow grew thicker, settling over both of us.

I wasn't thinking, I was just feeling. All the frustration, hurt, and shame that had been buried deep for such a long time flowed out of me and over Earl. The sensation changed from an icy pain to warmth. All I wanted was Earl back. I wanted to prove to him how sorry I was, and I'd never let him down again. I needed one more chance to give him a life he deserved.

A red glow swirled out of my fingers. It felt like my hand was too close to a naked flame. The glow moved from the top of Earl's head and slowly along his body. It kept in time with my hands as I moved them to the tip of Earl's tail. The glow drifted in the air and vanished.

The pain in my chest faded as Earl opened his eyes and drew in a breath.

Chapter 13

"Why am I soaking wet?" My wonderful, incredible furry angel blinked up at me.

I stared down at him, not believing what I was seeing. My heart raced, my vision blurred, and I found it hard to breathe. "You're alive?"

"And freezing but also weirdly hot. What's going on? Where are we?" Earl's eyes narrowed. "And where's that frog?" He stood, shook snow off his back, and staggered to the side.

I caught hold of him. "How do you feel?" I was too afraid to blink in case this wasn't real.

"Hold on. Something's not quite right." Earl backed away, making that uniquely gross sound only a cat can make when it's about to heave up an enormous ball of fur. A giant green slimy coil shot from his mouth and plopped onto the bed.

I quickly flipped it off the bed as it burned through the covers.

We both peered over the edge at the fizzling lump of evilness.

"A purple devil frog did that to you." I grabbed Earl and wrapped him in a tight hug.

"Gross. But I still have no idea what's going on. Why is it snowing? Are we in the hospital?"

I laughed. "I really don't know what's happening. My friends think I'm making it rain and snow inside, though. How are you back? How are you breathing? You died!"

He struggled out of my grip. "Back up a few steps. The last thing I remember, we were in Olympus's office, and I was tackling that slimy little intruder who kept spitting at Monty."

I nodded. "You saved me. You bit the poisonous frog. But... it killed you."

He lifted a paw. "I look alive now."

I laughed again. "You do! And I'm not sure why. Storm cast a stasis spell on you. But you've been dead for two days."

He wriggled about, flipping his tail and arching his back. "I'm definitely not. I feel good. Very much alive."

"Was it something I did that brought you back?" I couldn't stop running my hands over him, so overjoyed to have my familiar breathing again. "I got this hot sensation flood through me, and a red glow covered you."

"Maybe. I was dreaming about frogs and fighting. You were there. I got freezing and then roasting hot. And I was hearing your voice. You said you wanted me back."

"That's what I was concentrating on. I needed a chance to make things right between us. Earl, I have messed up big time."

His ears flicked. "I'm listening."

I caught him up in my arms like he was a baby. For once, he didn't object as I rocked him against my soggy chest. "I'm so sorry for shutting you out. I didn't realize how much it hurt you. And I didn't realize how much I'd miss not having you around until you were gone."

A snowflake settled on his nose, and he licked it off. "You always acted like you never needed me. It hurt."

"I know. I lost focus because I was so busy trying to make my magic fit in the bakery that I shut everything else out. It was a full-time job making sure I didn't mess up every day. It seems I didn't get that right with you."

The rain stopped, but the snow continued.

"Neither of us ever fit in at the bakery. Being there felt weird and unnatural. I only agreed to stay because, when we first found each other, we seemed like a good fit. Your magic had a weird vibe to it, but I always assumed you'd grow into your power. But it never manifested. And that meant my ability could never fully form." He snuggled against me. "I always felt like a defective familiar because I couldn't help you with what you needed."

"You never said anything to me."

"And there's a lot you've never said to me." If Earl had eyebrows, he'd be arching them. "I followed you when you went into the woods. I don't know what you're hiding there, but it's big, and you always smelled of strange magic when you came home."

I groaned. "It was my attempt at appearing normal. The only way I can keep my magic functioning is to take it from others. There are magic users living in a hidden house in the woods. That's where I go all the time. They donate their magic to me. I should have told you."

He wrinkled his nose. "That explains so much. When you'd come back from one of your secret outings, your magic would be all over the place. I'd try to tune in with you and strengthen our bond, but it was like having a different witch to work with. I never knew who I was getting. And then you came back one night with loads of weird, intensely dark magic. It kinda freaked me out. I wondered if someone had come into the bakery in disguise as you."

"That was probably after I drained Bram Vexx. He's a terrible guy, but I was desperate."

"The guy you pretended was your boyfriend?"

"Yes! How did you know about that?"

"When I'm not sleeping, I'm listening." Earl thumped my nose with a paw. "You have to stop. There's no way we'll ever have a proper witch familiar bond while you're doing this magic draining scam. Borrowed magic won't link with me. We won't connect with each other."

"But that's the only way I can get my baking magic to function. Well, half-function."

"Your magic is working fine if you're doing this." He looked around the snowy room.

"This magic will never fit in the bakery. What am I supposed to serve, snow cones and popsicles in an igloo?"

"Then we don't fit in the bakery. I don't know why your magic behaves like this, but this is something I can work with. This feels primal and natural. I've felt it before but only when you've had your guard down. This is your real magic."

I took a few seconds to consider his words. "Storm said this magic is like hers, but she's an elemental witch. That's definitely not me. I'm a Brimstone."

"We need to figure it out," Earl said. "But please, don't force me to stay at that bakery. I can't handle it any longer. Even being at Odessa's for a few days has made me feel better. I haven't had to hide under a haze of catnip to get through each day."

"I'm the reason you were always getting high on catnip?"

"It took the edge off. And I really wouldn't mind if I never saw another cake again."

I kissed his furry head. "You won't have to stay at the bakery. We're in this together. You're my familiar, and I love you." I looked around the room, which now looked more like the inside of a snow globe than a hospital room. My heart lurched, but it was an excited lurch, not one of fear. "I did this, but I really don't know how."

"Let me try something. If you're doing this, I can tap into it. I'll test our bond and see if my ability works better when you don't fake your magic." Earl flipped out of my arms, shook himself one more time, and moved to the end of the bed. He wriggled his nose. A swirl of snow shot up from the floor.

"Was that you?" I scrambled to the end of the bed and watched the snow dance around the room.

"Huh! Will you look at that? It was effortless when my power linked with you. I barely had to think about it. It just happened."

I shook my head. "But I'm supposed to bake."

The door opened, and I tensed as a nurse stepped inside.

She looked around the room, and her lips pursed. "What are you doing?"

I looked at Earl and grinned. "Honestly, I have no clue, but it feels amazing."

The nurse jammed her hands on her hips. "You're the one making it snow outside?"

"Um... I didn't know it was snowing outside."

"Then you need to look out the window. And stop messing with this room." The nurse twirled her finger in the air. "I'll sedate you if you don't behave."

"I'm not doing it deliberately. Well, I guess I am, but I need to learn how to make it stop."

"Please do. I have no intention of wearing snow boots inside the hospital." She stepped daintily across the snow. "How are you feeling?"

"Better than I've felt in a long time."

The nurse brushed a snowflake off her eyelashes then ran her hands over me. "You do seem remarkably well. Any aftereffects? The death of a familiar is always difficult."

"He's not dead. He's right here." I pointed at Earl.

She lowered her hands. "I thought that was the reason for your admission. Your friends said you collapsed after your familiar died."

"He was dead, but he's back now." I slid off the bed. "Is there any chance I can get out of here? I'm feeling fine."

"I can't force you to stay. But I should get the doctor to take a look at you before deciding if you need any further treatment."

"Can I discharge myself?"

"I wouldn't advise it."

"But I can?"

"Yes, if you must! Just let me get the doctor to give you the onceover."

"There's no need." I went to the door, and stopped. There was no way I'd be able to get past my friends and family. "Is there a back way out of here?"

The nurse shook her head. "No. Wait right here. And I want this snow stopped and gone by the time I return." She hurried out of the door.

I wasn't waiting around for the doctor. I had a dozen urgent things on my to-do list to deal with.

A quick peek out the door only confirmed everyone was waiting to see me. Backtracking, I headed to the window, happy to see I was on the street level. I grabbed my things out of the locker by the side of the bed and quickly changed.

"What's the plan?" Earl said.

"We need to find out how that frog got in Olympus's office. No one poisons my awesome familiar and gets away with it."

"Plus, we have a dead guy to consider."

"Two dead guys. And there could be more bodies if we don't hurry. That frog being there was no accident. Someone put it in the cell to kill Torin."

"And me! Although I think you're right. I wasn't the target."

I tickled under his chin. "No, but you are my hero."

"So, we're making an escape?" His whiskers twitched.

"Yep. Out the window. I can't handle everyone right now. My parents won't stop asking questions about what's going on, and I don't have answers."

"What about your friends? They'll help you, even though you've been deceiving them just like me."

"Not any more. And I'll welcome their help. But right now, I need space to clear my head and figure out what we're going to do next. Are you with me?"

"If you promise not to force me to pretend to love the bakery, or bakery magic, or donuts. Bleurgh! I hate those things. Greasy, super sweet blobs of nastiness."

A final blast of snow swirled around me before settling on the floor. "I promise, we'll find a way that works for both of us."

"Then let's get out of here."

I slid open the window then climbed out into snow.

Earl easily hopped through the window, almost disappearing as he landed, the snow was so deep.

I shook my head in amazement. "I really did this?"

"This had better not be all you can conjure up with your real magic."

"You don't like snow?"

"I like it more than muffins, I suppose."

"I'll get you some booties."

Earl growled. "You know what you can do with your cat booties."

I chuckled. "You'd look cute in a matching hat, scarf, and color coordinated booties. I'll get Gloria to knit you some sets."

"Who's Gloria?"

I scooped him up and settled him around my shoulders. "An amazing friend. I'll introduce you. I'll walk. You stay warm."

I'd only taken a dozen steps away from the hospital when I slowed. The back of my neck was prickling.

"We're being watched," Earl whispered.

I nodded. "I can sense it too. Can you see where they are?"

"There's a shady looking guy peeking out from behind a tree near the parking lot."

I narrowed my eyes as I focused on the guy. "It's Bram! What's he doing here?"

"Let's get him and find out."

Bram's head vanished behind the tree, but I knew he'd seen me. I raced through the snow. I'd never felt so alive. My power flowed effortlessly through me, clicking into place now I'd stopped hiding it.

"I can see him," Earl said. "We're closing in."

"Let's test out this weather magic." I thrust out my hands, and a blast of snow slammed into Bram's back. He staggered and crashed to the ground.

"Nice one. That worked," Earl said.

"Yeah! Did you feel it? It was amazing."

He booped my cheek with his damp nose.

Bram was getting to his hands and knees as we reached him. I planted my foot on his back and shoved him down in the snow. "Not so fast. We need to talk about arson."

"Get off me, you crazy witch!"

"You blew up the bakery while Uncle Albert and Earl were inside. You could have killed them."

"You had fair warning," he spluttered. "I gave you plenty of time to repay your debt. More than most."

I slammed another blast of snow against him.

"Quit doing that. It hurts. Where'd you borrow this magic from? Getting yourself in even more debt, I suppose."

"This is all mine." I held out my hands and grinned. "It belongs to me. It always has. And if you don't start talking about what you did to the bakery, you'll find yourself turned into a snowman. Or maybe an ice sculpture."

Bram shuddered as I pressed my foot down. "You still owe Sylvester. I'm here to collect."

"You took away everything I had by blowing up the bakery. What am I supposed to repay him with?" I lifted my foot and allowed him to roll over.

He scrambled away crablike across the snow. "How'd you get so powerful?"

"We were always this powerful," Earl said. "It just took Luna a little time to catch on."

Bram glowered at me. "Sylvester won't be happy when he learns you attacked me."

"And I'm not happy about losing the bakery. I'm also not happy about you endangering my family."

"I was following orders. Sylvester figured you needed a nudge."

I bared my teeth but kept my anger in check, partly to avoid making the deluge of snow blasting us any worse. "I'll admit, I was wrong to get into debt and not pay it back when I should. But Sylvester should never have ordered that attack. And you should never have done it."

His fear-filled gaze went to my hands. I glanced at them, and sparkles of brilliant white magic flickered off my skin like tiny, deadly looking shards of ice. I felt so powerful.

"The fire wasn't meant to be that intense," Bram stammered. "I got these magic blasts off a friend. He said they were more for show than anything else. He said to use them all because they were old and wouldn't be that powerful."

"The place was an inferno. And I was standing right outside. You knew what you were doing."

He lifted a shoulder. "You needed a warning."

"I got your warning loud and clear. Now, you get mine. I'll repay my debt but only what I owe. No interest added on, no favors owed to you, and no doubling the debt. I'll clear it, and then we're done."

"Sylvester won't like that."

"Then I'll go talk to him and make him see sense." I slammed a blast of snow into Bram's face.

He spluttered and swatted his hands in front of him. "Sure. Whatever you say."

"And you'll confess to arson. You'll tell the Magic Council what you did."

Bram shook his head. "I can't do that. They'll send me to jail."

"You deserve it. And find a better job when you get out, one that doesn't involve terrifying or stalking people."

"Maybe take up gardening," Earl said. "It's therapeutic."

Bram lifted his chin. "I won't confess. You can't make me."

"People have seen you around Witch Haven. You've been noticed lurking outside the bakery, and you're known to the Magic Council. They won't need to dig hard to link you to the arson. Maybe the friend who gave you those dodgy magic blasts might tell them he sold them to you. He won't want to be linked to an arson case that destroyed a store and almost killed someone."

"And an awesome familiar," Earl said.

I nodded. "I reckon he'll happily give up your name to avoid going to jail."

"He won't talk. We're buddies."

"Don't be so sure about that. And even if he doesn't talk, perhaps the Magic Council will speak to Sylvester and tell him you revealed his secrets to them. When they pin the arson attack on him, he might throw you under the bus."

Bram scowled at me. "Sylvester wouldn't do that." He didn't sound all that convinced.

"Are you willing to take that risk?" I gave him my sweetest smile. "And, of course, I could always set my fiancé on you. Cole Kellam has a score to settle with you."

He tipped his head back and sighed.

"How about you wait here and think about what you've done?"

"No way! I'm getting out of here. You're crazy." Bram lifted his hands. "And keep that magic away from me."

I poured ice over Bram, freezing him into place until he was a life-sized ice sculpture.

"Whoa! That was an epic spell," Earl said. "I felt it vibrate to my toe pads. They're all tingly."

I stood over a frozen Bram. "Every time I use this magic, I feel energized. I never believed Uncle Albert when he said using his baking magic made him feel good. Whenever I tried it, I got a headache and an intense feeling of failure."

"Not anymore," Earl said. "This feels great."

I tickled his head. "It does. We'll let the Magic Council deal with Bram. Maybe being stuck in ice for a while will make him reconsider his career options."

A branch breaking under someone's foot had me whirling around. My mom stood in front of me.

"Luna, we need to talk."

Chapter 14

"Oh! Hey, Mom. Did the nurse tell you I was gone?" I tried to hide what I'd done to Bram, but he was almost twice the size of me and encased in a huge block of ice.

"I checked your room and saw the open window. I climbed through and followed the tracks in the snow." Mom took a step closer. "I also saw the snow and water in the hospital room. Was that all your doing?"

"Possibly. I can't really talk now, though. Someone hurt Earl, and there's a killer to stop."

"Wait! I know you're busy and you want to help people, but this can't wait any longer." Her gaze went to Bram. "What you just did was incredible. I never knew you were so powerful."

I bit my bottom lip. "You saw that?"

She nodded. "Have you always had weather magic?"

"No. Maybe. I don't know. I'm not that powerful with baking spells. And that's something I do want to talk to you about, but I can't now." I had no clue how to reveal that I couldn't bake to save my life, and if I never touched a mixing bowl again, I'd be happy.

Mom lifted a hand, and her bottom lip wobbled. "I didn't know."

The painful note in her voice made me hesitate. "What are you talking about?"

"I often wondered if your baking ability wouldn't be as strong as mine, but I hoped you'd get by. And Albert was always there to support you. I didn't think I had anything to worry about."

"You've lost me. Mom, I really have to go. I need to tell the Magic Council about this guy trapped in the ice. And the treasure hunters are vulnerable. The killer could still be after them."

"No, just listen." She walked through the snow until we were face-to-face. "I don't visit enough."

"That's okay. Work keeps you busy, and you love your baking."

"It's not that. I don't visit because I feel guilty. I made a mistake. No, I didn't. What happened meant I got you."

I shook my head. "You're not making any sense."

Mom looked at the ground. "I had an affair with a weather warlock. And you resulted from that affair."

My jaw dropped, and a swirl of snow spun around me. "You cheated on Dad?"

"It's not something I'm proud of."

"Does he know?"

"I've never told him, but he most likely suspects something happened. It was a long time ago, and nothing like that has happened since. It was one night, when I was young and foolish."

"Why did you do it?"

Her gaze remained lowered. "Your father was never around. We're both ambitious, but he took things to another level. He accepted a year-long job at the opposite end of the country without even consulting me. We'd barely been married five minutes, and he was leaving. I knew there'd be times when we'd have to be apart, but it was for a whole year, and we had plans to start a family. He said I'd have to get used to it. Baking came first. Your father told me it was the only thing he truly loved. It just about broke my heart."

I wasn't sure how I felt. Angry? Confused? Sad for how lousy their marriage must be? All this time, they'd had this huge secret lodged between them, and I was a part of it.

"You should have told Dad. And you shouldn't have cheated on him," I finally said.

"I was young and angry. I deeply regret it. But I can't be sad because I became pregnant with you. Your father didn't even think it was strange. We were newlyweds, so there were no problems in that department when he was around, but he never questioned the dates of your conception. And I was so happy when I had you. You were a perfect baby, always smiling and content."

"My dad's not my real dad, though. Why did you never tell me?"

"He is! And Galahad loves you. You're his daughter, even though you're not biologically his."

"Would he have done that if he knew the truth about me? And you."

"Of course." Mom didn't hesitate. "Underneath the career obsession, he has a warm heart. He just sometimes forgets to look up from the mixing bowl and see what a fabulous life he has with us."

"What about the other guy? Does he know about me?"

"No, I broke off contact as soon as I found out I was pregnant. I didn't want to ruin the marriage. I loved your father."

"Loved? You don't anymore?"

Mom twisted her fingers together, the skin pink from the cold. "It's complicated. We're both older and wiser and have forged our own paths in life. Honestly, it barely feels like I'm married to him."

"So why not leave him?"

"Because... lots of reasons. We wanted to give you a stable home life."

"I had that living at Fandango's." The words came out sharp, but I had every right to be angry.

Mom bit her lip. "Yes, you did. But we also have the family reputation to consider. If we split, we'd yank apart our strong position. And we want to be at the top in a few years' time."

I snorted my disbelief. "That would make you truly happy? You'd rather stay with a man you don't care about because of that?"

"I do care for him. But reputation and status is everything in this business."

"Then I'm glad I'm not a part of it. You must both be miserable." I was taking my rage out on my mom, and I could see my words were stinging harder than the freezing snow, but I couldn't keep them inside. I'd just found out my family had been living one big lie.

"I'm so sorry. I didn't realize your baking magic was affected by what I'd done. You never said anything."

"Just like you never said anything about my real dad. Of course it was going to affect me. I have half the power I should, mixed in with weather magic." Every time I moved my hands, more snow was picked up and tossed around.

"I thought my baking magic would be your dominant power. And you've been working with Albert all these years, and the bakery is so successful. I assumed everything worked out for the best."

"It worked out because of him. Uncle Albert's been doing the heavy lifting all these years. And he's been covering for me. He knew there was a problem but was always too kind to question me about it too much." I huffed out a frozen breath. "And this is the main reason I've been so reluctant to work with either you or Dad."

"But I could have helped. Which is why you should work with me. Your father doesn't need to know anything about this."

I shook my head. "All this time, I've been thinking it was me. I thought my magic was faulty, and I was broken. A magical blunt."

My mom reached for me, but I stepped out of her way. I wasn't ready to hug and forgive just yet. "I should have done better for you. Paid you more attention and seen you were struggling."

I threw my hands up and snow spun around me. "It all makes sense. Witch Haven has been experiencing strange weather, and it's because of me. I've caused high winds, tornadoes, and lightning storms. People got hurt. There's been so much damage. And I had no idea because I wasn't in control of my ability. I didn't know I had this ability."

A tear trickled down my mom's cheek. "I didn't know things were so bad for you."

Sadness made my heart stutter. "You focused on your work and assumed everything was fine. But I've been struggling and so worried there was something wrong with me. And I've done dumb things to hide what I thought were my failings. They got me in trouble."

"And that's my fault. I felt so guilty about what happened but then blissfully happy because I got you. I love you more than anything."

"More than your baking career?"

"Of course I do. But yes, that's important to me. As you know, baking is a passion we have no choice but to follow." Mom sucked in a breath. "Sorry, that was thoughtless of me. You don't know that. I'd always assumed you had the same passion for baking as me and your father. I never understood your reluctance to expand your opportunities."

"Now you know why. I'm more weather witch than anything else. I'm guessing the warlock you cheated with must have been powerful."

Mom nodded slowly, her gaze flickering from me to the ground, as if too ashamed to meet my gaze. "He must have been. He was a charming man. We didn't really discuss our powers, but I knew he was strong." She held her hand out to me. "I had a moment of weakness during a difficult period when

I was young and didn't know any better. Can you forgive me?"

I stared at her outstretched hand. I wasn't sure I could. This was a shock, but it fit everything into place. It was no wonder I was having so much trouble making my baking magic work. It had always felt unnatural and weak because I'd inherited some of my biological dad's ability. And all this time, I'd been messing with Witch Haven. I'd caused the lightning storm that blasted the huge oak tree through the library window and injured Cole. I'd almost helped a killer get away with murder when I'd conjured tornadoes and thrown them at the village. And now this. The blizzard showed no signs of stopping. And I didn't want it to. This insanely intense weather matched my emotions perfectly.

Earl leaped off my shoulders and flipped in the air. He created a life-sized snow cat with the flick of a paw. "I see no drawbacks to this magic. I finally have my full powers, and they're awesome."

I grudgingly admitted it felt amazing to find magic that suited me, but I wasn't ready to forgive my mom for hiding this secret for such a long time.

"Luna, tell me what to do to make this right," my mom said.

"I'm not sure you can."

"I know what I'm going to do. I plan to use this new power to zap whoever planted that devil frog I chewed on," Earl said. "I can still taste that gross little critter in my mouth."

"Come with me. We can talk about this," my mom said. "I can tell you about your biological father if you'd like to know more about him."

"I thought you only spent a night with him. You can't know that much."

"True, but it was an intense night."

I wrinkled my nose. "I'm not sure I want to know." I considered the man who raised me my true dad. Sure, there were times when he'd stayed away, but I now understood why he wasn't always around. He must have known something was off with my magic. He could even have had concerns I was his child. It was no surprise he'd put a barrier between us.

"Please, Luna. I have to find a way to make this up to you."

"I need time to process. And Earl's right, there are other things going on. We will talk, but I need to visit the treasure hunters. They could be in danger if someone is out to get them. Two of them are already dead."

"Don't do that. It sounds dangerous. The Magic Council will deal with that problem."

"It's my problem. I'm involved. Earl died because of what's going on."

"But it's not safe. What if the killer comes for you because you're getting close to finding out who it is? Stay with me. We'll go back to the hospital and talk to everyone."

I hesitated. "Are you going to tell Dad what happened? Will you tell him I'm not really his daughter?"

She chewed on her bottom lip for a few seconds. "I will. I want no more secrets. Hiding this truth from you and your father has led to this mess. I was selfish. I didn't realize how much you were struggling or how unhappy you were. I should have done better. I've failed you."

I didn't correct her. Mom had let me down. All these years trying to figure out what was wrong with me, and it turned out I was fitting a square magical spell into a round magical hole.

"We will deal with this but one problem at a time. Go back to Odessa's farmhouse, and I'll meet you there later."

Mom pursed her lips and then nodded. "Be careful. I really do love you. I just made a mistake. Building the perfect family is more complicated than making the perfect sweet flan."

"Families aren't like cake. You don't make it and then let it get eaten. You always have to put in the work. That never stops." Mom had made a huge mistake, and I was wounded by her lie.

I turned and traipsed away through the snow, Earl hopping back on my shoulders to avoid getting frozen paws.

Poisonous frogs and a murderer on the loose seemed easier to deal with than an adulterous parent.

Chapter 15

"Should we try this new magic some more?" I said to Earl as I put distance between me and my mom.

"I've already been trying it. I can't stop. Look behind you."

I turned and saw a series of small snowmen in a loopy row he'd created as we'd walked along. Some sat at a jaunty angle, a few had bulbous heads, and he'd even conjured up a few stick arms. "They look good."

"I know. Where are we headed?"

"To find Elsa and Reuben. One of them could be our killer. And even if they aren't, they could both be the killer's next target."

"Or the curse's next target."

"Yep. We need to get them somewhere secure and find out the truth."

"What do you want to do?"

"A location spell. Can you give me a furry hand with that?"

"Sure. It should be easy now we know what we're doing and not blundering around with buttercream and baklava." He wrapped himself around my shoulders. "I'm ready when you are. And just so you know, I was paying attention back there. What your mom did sucked. She should have told you the truth."

"I don't disagree."

"But she was also young and passionate. Your dad wasn't looking after her right."

"So that makes it okay to cheat?"

"Never. But... if she hadn't cheated, you wouldn't be here, and I wouldn't be your amazing snowman creating familiar."

My hands clenched, but I nodded. "I'm thinking it all through."

"And she's not the only one in the family who's got a knack for hiding the truth."

"My reasons for hiding things are totally different."

"But you hid a lot. And people, mainly me, got messed up because of it. Maybe take it easy on her. You know how easy it is to let a lie get away with you."

"I'm still thinking."

"Well, if you want to do any actual talking about it, I'm right here."

I petted his side. "And I'm glad to have you here. Let's do some magic." I took a deep breath and hesitated. I'd always felt fearful whenever I'd used my magic, never certain of what would come out, but this was different. I was a weather witch and a powerful one. Although I still wasn't certain how to switch off this snow, it wasn't making me tired. I felt truly alive for the first time in years.

It helped to have a map and something to guide the spell when searching for someone, but I had none of that to hand. It was time to see what I could do with just my magic and my amazing familiar. I simply stretched out my fingers, wiggled them, and imagined seeing Elsa and Reuben.

It happened effortlessly, and I got an image of them at Odessa's farmhouse loading their tents into Killian's truck. "I know where to go."

"Me, too. I saw inside your head. How weird is that?"

"You're not going to see all my thoughts, are you?"

He grimaced. "I really hope not. I expect you spend most of your thinking power drooling over Cole. Let's go find out who planted that frog and make them sorry for ever messing with us."

We dashed to the farmhouse, the snow now several feet deep. Even though I should have been freezing, I had an internal warmth that was making me glow. My toes weren't even cold, and I was wearing only basic boots and thin socks.

We reached Odessa's farmhouse, and I hurried around the side to the barns. Elsa, Reuben, and Killian were just finishing putting things in the back of his truck.

One person who I hadn't seen in my location spell was Devlin Goody. He stood beside the truck, talking to Reuben.

I wasn't thrilled to see him, but he had a job to do. Although he wasn't doing it that well since he hadn't caught the killer. But maybe I could help him solve that puzzle.

Elsa raised a hand when she saw me. "I'm glad to see you up and about. We heard what happened with that poisonous frog." Her gaze went to Earl. "You're both okay? I heard your familiar died."

I nodded. "We are now. It looks like you're leaving."

Killian strolled over and tucked a pack into the back of the truck. "They've decided it's too dangerous to stay. I don't disagree. This curse wants the treasure hunters dead. I never thought it was real, but after what happened to Torin, even I'm convinced there's something to it."

"Luna, what are you doing here?" Devlin strode over with Reuben beside him. "I thought you were in the hospital."

"I got better. You haven't closed the case, have you? That purple devil frog was planted in the cell."

He tsked at me. "Of course I haven't. And I'm well aware those frogs don't usually live in Olympus's office."

"Have you found out what happened? How did it get in there?" I glanced at Elsa and Reuben.

"That's none of your business," Devlin said.

"It's okay. Luna's been great to us while we've been camping," Reuben said. "Devlin was just giving us an update. They didn't find anything in the office, and there was nothing suspicious in the cell. It's so weird."

"So how did that purple devil frog get to Torin?" I said.

Reuben scrubbed his chin. "Maybe it got inside his jacket. It could have crept in there for a sleep and woke when Torin was put in the cell. He could have put a hand in his pocket and touched it."

"You believe his death was just bad luck? Like the explosion that injured him?"

"Luna, don't you have somewhere else to be?" Devlin muttered.

I crossed my arms over my chest and smiled at him. "No, I'm good right here."

"Torin was a decent guy," Reuben said, "just like Alaric. I can't believe anyone would do this deliberately."

"That's enough," Devlin said. "This is an ongoing investigation, and we don't need any outside interference from nosy amateurs."

"I'm not interfering, but I'm involved in these murders. I was there when Torin's body was found, and Earl caught the frog. You might never have known what happened to Torin if he hadn't done that."

"I accept payment in all dried meats. Steamed mackerel is also acceptable," Earl said.

"Your assistance is greatly appreciated." Devlin spoke through gritted teeth. "Now go."

Reuben shook his head. "Torin thought he'd be safe inside that cell. It must have been why he got himself arrested. You'd think the Magic Council could have protected him."

"He didn't get himself arrested. He assaulted me." Devlin touched his still swollen nose. "And we always protect people in danger."

"Sure, but he only hit you to stay safe. He was never a violent guy."

"It's this curse," Elsa said. "That's what it has to be. Everything feels strange and unsettling."

"Why are you so sure it's the curse doing this and not an actual person?" I said.

"Luna, now's not the time," Devlin said.

Elsa sighed. "It doesn't matter if Luna knows."

My grin was possibly a touch on the smug side as I flashed it Devlin's way. "Go on."

"We thought Torin and Alaric had found the gem. Both of them were being secretive just before they died. They were trying to shut us out. We got worried."

"You think the curse activated because they actually found the treasure everyone's been searching for all these years?" I said.

Killian nodded. "I reckon that's what happened. And Alaric was a smart guy. He could have done his own search with Torin, and they located the gem. They decided to share the power between themselves and exclude Elsa and Reuben, but it backfired."

"That makes no sense. If they had the gem, they'd be impossible to kill."

"Only if you believe the immortality power theory," Reuben said. "Maybe they didn't use it, or it didn't work that way."

"Or they didn't get a chance to use it for anything," Elsa said, "or one of them stole the gem from the other. Getting all that power would go to a person's head."

"If they found the gem, it gives both of you a motive for wanting them dead," I said. "You must have been angry they'd gone back on their word. Weren't you supposed to share the gem's power equally?"

"It gives us a motive, but that doesn't mean we did it," Elsa said. "We weren't anywhere near Torin when the explosion happened in the cave, and I was with Reuben when Alaric was stabbed. And then there's the purple devil frog. How would we have managed that? I don't have the power to control animals."

"Reuben suggested the frog crept into Torin's jacket," I said.

He nodded. "I don't know much about frogs, but why not? They like dark places, and Torin was always leaving his jacket lying around. He was messy."

I turned to Reuben. "Maybe the frog was planted in the jacket when you realized Torin's plan to exclude you from getting access to the gem's power."

Reuben raised a hand. "Hold on. I didn't kill Torin with a frog!"

"You slipped it into his pocket before he left the camp to get help from the Magic Council."

"No! Not true. I wouldn't do that."

"You're not helping, Luna," Devlin said, but his eyes were narrowed as he studied Reuben.

"How would I have been able to handle that frog without being poisoned?" Reuben licked his lips as his gaze darted from me to Devlin. "I didn't even know those things lived in the woods. If I did, I wouldn't have been so quick to stomp around looking for the gem, knowing they could have leaped on me."

"They're rare," Killian said. "It's unlikely you'd find one unless you were searching for it."

My brow furrowed. Reuben had made a valid point about avoiding being poisoned.

"Thank you for your input, Luna, but I have a handle on things. It's why I'm here." Devlin turned to Elsa. "I've been checking your background."

Her eyebrows shot up. "You have?"

A self-satisfied look crossed Devlin's face. "You haven't been honest with me."

"You know all about me."

"That's not true. When I checked your records, there were anomalies. Even your address is false. Why would that be, unless you have something to hide?"

Her gaze shot around the group. "It's not what you think. I didn't kill Alaric or Torin."

I stared at Devlin in open-mouthed surprise. Had he uncovered the killer? Devlin actually knew how to do his job!

"Explain why you gave me a false statement," Devlin said. "There are gaps in your education history, your address wasn't real, and as for your employment record, it wasn't that hard to discover it was also false."

Elsa sucked in a deep breath. "Maybe I wasn't truthful about all of that, but it's not relevant to what's happening here."

"So why lie?" I said.

Devlin nodded. "Yes, what are you hiding? Did you come here to secure the gem and have been targeting the other treasure hunters until only you remain? You used the fictitious curse as a cover to get away with murder."

"I didn't do that."

"Have you found the gem?" I tensed. If Elsa had that kind of power in her possession, she'd be unstoppable.

"No! I haven't found it. I figured Torin and Alaric had it." She scrubbed at her forehead. "They were being so secretive. They had to be hiding something important."

Reuben frowned at her. "What's going on, Elsa? Why the lies?"

"You need to come with me for further questioning," Devlin said. "There's something suspicious about your story. You're here under false pretenses, and I intend to find out why."

Elsa backed away. Was she going to make a run for it?

I held up my hands, ready to blast her with magic.

She stopped when she saw the magic sparking on my fingers and sighed. "I'm not the killer. But I did lie to you. I'm an undercover agent working for the Magic Council." She reached into her inside jacket pocket and flashed her credentials.

"The Magic Council has undercover agents?" I lowered my hands. "Like spies?"

"Why didn't I know about this?" Devlin's cheeks glowed. "The Magic Council should have told me they had an agent in the area."

"That defeats the point of it being undercover," Earl said.

Elsa nodded. "This had to be a discreet operation. The fewer people who knew, the better."

"You're not really a treasure hunter?" Reuben said.

"It's what I specialize in, but I don't treasure hunt for personal gain." She slid her credentials back into her pocket. "I work with the Magic Council to secure rare and powerful magical artefacts. There's dangerous stuff out there, and we make sure it doesn't get into the wrong hands."

"We wouldn't have done any harm with the gem," Reuben said.

"You can't guarantee that. If half of what the legend states about that gem is true, it's too powerful for most magic users to control. It would have consumed you. You'd have been forced to do its bidding and harmed a lot of people."

"Two people have already been harmed," I said. "Do you think Alaric and Torin's murder have to do with this gem? You really believe in it?"

Elsa pursed her lips. "We follow-up all leads when it comes to powerful items like this, and there's plenty of historical evidence to suggest this gem was once real. It might no longer exist, but there's enough information to support the belief it's more than a myth." She glanced at Reuben. "I didn't mean to deceive you, and I've enjoyed working with you, but you were getting too close to the truth."

"How did you even know they were hunting for the gem?" I asked.

"We monitor all activity relating to magic treasure hunting. Most of the time, it's enthusiastic amateurs, and we don't worry about them. But this group was onto something. Alaric was highly intelligent, and he'd located information sources we didn't even know existed."

Reuben nodded, although he didn't look all that happy about being lied to by Elsa. "The guy was relentless when he found a lead. He spent hours hunting in dusty libraries for clues."

"We tracked Alaric's plans and the work he'd done and inserted an operative on the trip. We needed to make sure, if the gem was discovered, it would be safely taken and stored where it couldn't be misused," Elsa said.

"I should still have been told," Devlin grumbled. "You've made me look like a fool, and we've wasted time interviewing you and doing background checks."

I almost felt sorry for him. Devlin had been convinced he'd found the killer, yet this whole time, Elsa was working for the same organization as him.

"I had to keep up the pretense, or my cover would have been blown." Elsa didn't sound apologetic for messing with Devlin.

My stomach jolted as I turned to Reuben. "With Alaric dead, Torin poisoned, and you working with the Magic Council, that leaves only one person who could be the killer."

Reuben made a strange squeaking sound. "You can't think it was me. We're all convinced the gem curse is killing us. That's why we're leaving. We want out of here. And I want nothing to do with that gem. Even if there wasn't a curse associated with it, it sounds too powerful for me to handle."

"As Elsa said, power has a bad effect on people. Is that what's happening to you?" The snow blew around me, and I directed it at Reuben.

"I know my limits. I don't want to be destroyed by the gem's power. I came on this trip for some fun. I didn't expect to be in the middle of two murder investigations and then accused of being the killer."

I glared at him. "It has to be you. You killed Torin, stabbed Alaric, and you poisoned Earl."

Reuben's forehead wrinkled. "Who's Earl?"

"I'm Earl. And you're a jerk." Earl hissed at Reuben. "You're going to pay for what you did to me. Poisonous frogs taste like one of Luna's soggy scones."

"Thanks for that."

Reuben's gaze flashed to Devlin. "I didn't do this. Call this witch off."

I shoved past Devlin before he had a chance to speak, anger making me see red. "You're not getting away with this. You poisoned my familiar, and now you're going to pay."

Chapter 16

My hands were raised, snow spinning around me in a violent flurry as I directed my rage and frustration at Reuben.

He scurried back, his hands lifted to keep the snow out of his eyes. "It wasn't me. It couldn't have been me. I didn't stab Alaric. And Torin was in a locked cell. There was no way for me to get to him."

"There's no one else. It must have been you." A shaft of ice ricocheted out of my chest and slammed into the dirt, an inch from Reuben's feet, making him leap back.

"Luna, you need to stop this," Devlin yelled above the roar of snow and wind. "I... I'm in charge here. I'll deal with Reuben if he is the killer."

I wasn't just angry at Reuben for what happened to Earl, but all the frustration and disappointment I'd felt over the years was rocketing through me. My failed magic, my mom's lies, my horrendous attempts at baking, murders in my beautiful village, and even Devlin being a major jerk to me.

The snow flurries grew intense as I channeled my fury at Reuben. "Admit you killed Alaric and Torin."

His mouth opened and closed several times. "But I didn't. I was with Elsa when Alaric was stabbed, and I didn't know about Torin until after he'd been poisoned. And I know nothing about poisonous frogs. I couldn't tell you what ones are harmful and what ones are just... froggy."

"Luna, I insist you stop this instant." Devlin's hat blew off his head and sailed away. "How are you even doing this kind of magic?"

"Because I can. And we have to stop a killer from getting away."

"And I will. You need to stay out of this." He attempted to push through the snow swirls protecting me but got shoved back and landed on his butt in a snowdrift.

"Confess!" I yelled at Reuben. "Did you find the gem and decide to keep it for yourself?"

He spluttered out a few half-words as he shoved huge icy snowflakes out of his eyes. "I promise, I'm no killer. I'm certain it was the curse. We got too close, and it decided to stop us. The gem doesn't want to be found. And if we stay, we're both dead." Reuben gestured at Elsa. "I just want this over with. I wish I'd never come to Witch Haven."

"I believe him," Elsa said. "Reuben was with me the night of Alaric's stabbing. We sat around the fire and had a few drinks. We talked about the gem. He couldn't have done it."

"Reuben must have left you at some point."

"Not for long enough to commit a murder. It's not possible. You're looking in the wrong place."

Devlin scrambled to his feet. "Luna Brimstone! I'll arrest you for the misuse of magic if you keep this up. I always knew your powers were unnatural. This display proves it."

I glared at him, and he visibly trembled as a giant snowball formed and hovered in the air in front of his face. "I'm not unnatural. This is my magic. All of this is me. I can bury you under this snow if I want to, and you wouldn't be able to stop me. I should. You've been a giant pain in my behind for too long, and you never gave me a chance to show I was a good witch."

"Do it," Earl said. "This guy's a jerk. And he wanted to shut the bakery and put Albert out of business. Smack him in the pie hole with that snowball."

I nodded. "Devlin, you've prodded, questioned, and assumed the worst about me for weeks, when all I was trying to do was get on with my life. I never wanted trouble. I was just doing my best. But you always thought I was bad news. You're wrong. I'm perfect. My magic is perfect. So is my familiar. And you need to leave me alone."

Devlin blinked rapidly as he looked around. "This... is all your magic?"

"I learned something about myself recently. I'm not a baker. And you were right about my magic. I was trying to do something I shouldn't. That was wrong, but I didn't know any better. Now I do." I flicked my wrists and whipped the snow into a frenzy. "And I'm using my magic to take down this killer."

He held up his hands, his eyes almost shut against the blizzard that slammed into him. "Let me do it. Let me take Reuben in and question him."

"You'll only let him go."

"I won't! And I agree with you. He's the only one who could have committed these murders."

"It wasn't him," Elsa protested. "I was with Reuben. You're both making a mistake."

I wasn't. I was sure about that. I'd never been more sure of anything in my whole life.

"Luna, you must calm down." Devlin threw himself through the snow and grabbed my elbow. "You did it. You solved the case. No one else needs to die."

A little of my rage faded, and the snow stopped swirling. "You really believe me?"

Devlin brushed snow off his shoulders and head. "I do. I'll take the suspect to the holding cell and question him. I'll get to the bottom of this."

"Can I be in on that interrogation?"

He tilted his head, and his eyes narrowed. "Don't push your luck. And we're having words about this new weather magic. If you're really behind this, you should be nowhere near the bakery making food for customers."

"I won't fight you on that." I lowered my hands, and the magic drew back inside me in a chilly wave.

"You should let the whole bakery glitch issue drop," Earl said. "Luna's just solved your case. And it isn't the first time she's helped you when you got your clues the wrong way around. Give her a gold star rather than a telling off."

"I'll pass on the gold star. I just want to see justice done," I said.

"You won't achieve that by arresting me," Reuben grumbled. "You're both wrong about me."

"Come with me," Devlin said. "You have questions to answer about the murders of Torin and Alaric."

Reuben didn't resist as Devlin caught hold of him. He looked defeated, and so he should. He'd finally been caught.

Devlin secured Reuben, nodded at me, and they blinked out of sight.

Elsa stared at me and then at the snow lying in huge heaps around us. "You're a really powerful weather witch. I don't think I've ever met anyone so strong."

Flexing my hands, I grinned. "I'm getting used to it. And I've just figured it out for myself. Do you really work for the Magic Council?"

She nodded. "I'm freelance. They bring me in on the tricky cases. But this is the first case I've been on that's involved murder to get to a treasure. Although I've witnessed plenty of fights when people think they're about to get wealthy with their discovery. Power and greed make people ugly."

"It looks like it did with Reuben."

Elsa didn't respond. She looked pensive and unhappy.

"I guess that means you can leave. If no one in the group found the gem, you won't keep looking for it, will you?"

Concern crossed her face. "I'll stick around. I still think Reuben's innocent."

"So... the curse did it?"

Elsa shrugged. "What else could it be?"

"What do you want me to do with your camping stuff?" Killian had wisely kept his head down during the confrontation.

Elsa turned to the truck. "If it's okay with Odessa, we can store the stuff in her barn. I don't mind sleeping out here. And I want to talk to Devlin when he's calmed down. I don't want him charging the wrong guy with murder."

"I don't mind driving you home," Killian said. "It'll be cold camping out with all this snow."

"I can deal with that," I said. "Let's see if we can warm things up."

Earl twitched his tail, leaped in the air, and scampered around, the snow underneath his paws melting away.

"Whatever you want," Killian said. "You're my only client, so I'll be around if you change your mind."

She shook her head. "Something strange is going on here. And I need to report in to the Magic Council. Would you mind unloading the gear?"

"Sure thing. Happy to help." He tugged out the first load of equipment.

"I'll go inside and make some calls." Elsa hurried away.

"Should we have a huge mug of celebratory hot chocolate, Earl?" I looked around when he didn't respond. "Earl? Where'd you go?"

I spotted his small furry black shape skulking across the melting snow. His ears were down, and he was almost flat on his stomach. "Hey, no chasing things."

Killian returned to get more equipment out of his truck. "How come you can suddenly do weather magic? I thought you baked."

"It's a long story. But safe to say, I won't be making any more desserts at Fandango's."

"But your uncle is going to get the place open again, isn't he? I love stopping by to grab a pastry. I've never had anything like them. They're so good."

"That's the plan. And he'll still be in charge. Although he might hire an assistant now I'm no longer a part of the business." There was still a lot to figure out, but I could focus on my future now we'd caught the killer.

"What are you gonna do if you're not working there?"

"That's a really good question." And right now, I had no answer.

There was a squeak, and a few seconds later, Earl trotted back with something hanging out of his mouth. I spotted a long tail and a small leg.

"Haven't you learned your lesson about not grabbing potentially poisonous things?" I held out my hand. "Give it to me. And don't bite it."

Earl spat his find into my hand. It was a small, pale yellow newt with black dots all over it. It didn't look injured, although it was doing a great job of playing dead.

Killian raced over and scooped it out of my hand. "No way! This is a silver tongued newt. They're a protected species. I didn't realize they'd gotten out this far."

"You've seen these newts before?"

"Sure. There's been occasional sightings in the woods. I thought this environment would be too dry for them, though." He glanced at the melting snow.

"Maybe all this weird weather meant they've been looking for safe havens."

"Sorry, Mr. Newt. I didn't mean to chase you out of your home. Things will be back to normal soon," I said.

"I still get to eat it, though, right?" Earl said. "I found it. I hunted it down. It's mine. Does newt taste good?"

Killian shook his head. "You shouldn't eat this one. It's incredibly rare."

"But it's mine. I could add some hot sauce if it's bland tasting."

"Earl, we don't eat the endangered wildlife. Go in the farmhouse and find some beef jerky," I said.

He grumbled a few times then turned and strutted away through the snow.

"Sorry about that. We're both excited about coming into our real powers. And Earl's got a lot of energy to burn off now he's not constantly stoned on catnip."

Killian was focused on the newt. "It's all good. He didn't hurt this little guy, just gave him a scare."

"You really love your animals, don't you?"

"Sure. I mean, what's not to love? And they need looking after. As Witch Haven gets more popular, some of the vulnerable animals suffer. I can never look away when an animal needs help. Sometimes, people aren't all that nice to them, so I need to look out for the little guys."

"I couldn't agree more. What are you going to do with this newt, though? Do they take them at the animal sanctuary?"

"No, but I volunteer for a group that protects rare species like this. I'll record some details and take photographs and send them the information." He lifted the newt onto his palm. "It would be great to get a thriving breeding colony around here. Imagine that, a load of these little guys running around the woods."

"And they're definitely not poisonous? Those spots remind me of the purple devil frog that hurt Earl."

Killian grinned and shook his head. "They're fine. Nothing bad will happen to us because we touched it. Although they secrete a foul tasting mucus as a defense response. Earl's lucky he didn't get a mouthful of something gross."

"He'll be grateful for that." I looked around, happy to see the snow already melting as the day heated. I was barely thinking about it, and my magic was responding.

"I'll find something to store this little guy in, then I'd better get the rest of the gear unpacked," Killian said.

I nodded. My amazing new weather magic had been raging non-stop, and it was time for a break, a very long lunch, then a nap. After that, I had the unwelcome task of speaking to my parents.

Chapter 17

I padded down the stairs, patting my sleep messy hair into some kind of style. I'd gotten a solid five hours of undisturbed sleep following Reuben's arrest.

I'd put a sign on my bedroom door, warning people not to disturb me unless the place was on fire or someone else was dead. I'd also wedged a chair under the door handle in case anyone felt like taking the risk of disturbing me. And it had worked. I'd curled up with Earl on my bed, and we'd crashed.

Wandering into the kitchen with Earl wrapped around my shoulders, I smiled when I found Odessa and Cole sitting at the kitchen table.

Cole had an empty plate of food in front of him, and Odessa was topping up his coffee.

"You're right on time. I've just pulled out a fresh batch of pumpkin spiced caramel muffins." She pulled out a seat for me, and I sank into it next to Cole.

"Sorry for running out on you all at the hospital," I said. "I had a lot to think about, and it got a bit intense."

"Everyone needs a little space now and again," Cole said. "How's the thinking going?"

"So far, so good. You're not mad at me for pulling a vanishing act?"

He shook his head. "Of course not. And I stopped by and saw your..." He raised his eyebrows and looked at Odessa.

"It's okay. I'm done with keeping secrets. I'm not hiding anything else ever again. It only got me into this huge mess. And it'll take some time to unpick it all."

Cole nodded. "Well, everyone at the farmhouse is doing fine. They were worried about you, but I grabbed them some food and told them you'd drop by as soon as you could."

I kissed his cheek. "Thanks, Cole. I appreciate your help."

"That's what all good fiancés are for." Odessa settled in the seat opposite me and placed a huge plate of delicious smelling muffins on the table. "What's this about a farmhouse?"

"My secret harem. I mentioned them in the hospital."

"Oh! Yes. Your harem." She flashed her eyebrows up. "I'll have to meet them soon. Everyone have a muffin." Odessa was so wonderfully non-judgmental about my big old mess.

I leaned over and hugged her. "I don't tell you enough what an amazing friend you are."

She giggled. "You're not so bad yourself. Now, eat up."

We all took muffins, and no one spoke for several minutes as we enjoyed the treats.

"I heard about Reuben's arrest," Odessa said. "I've been itching to come up and ask you about it, but Cole said you must need the rest."

He got another kiss for making sure I had such a great sleep. "Despite him protesting his innocence, Reuben must have killed Torin and Alaric. There was no one else left who could have done it," I said.

"Unless you believe in the gem curse."

"Which I don't. Have there been any updates while I've been sleeping?"

"Indigo dropped by a couple of hours ago. Apparently, Reuben is refusing to confess to either murder."

"He can't hold out much longer. He'll talk."

"Devlin's holding him overnight. Olympus is also overseeing things and asked Killian to bring in fresh clothes and toiletries for Reuben. They have no plans to let him go until he confesses."

"Is Elsa still around? She said she'd stay here until the case was solved."

Cole nodded. "She's not happy about Reuben's arrest. The last time I saw her, she was headed to the Magic Council to speak to someone in charge."

"Good luck with that. And she's definitely legit? Elsa flashed some credentials to show she worked with the Magic Council, but it all happened so fast."

"She checked out. Elsa was undercover to keep an eye on the group and see if they found anything related to the gem," Cole said.

"Maybe there really is treasure out there if the Magic Council is so interested," I said.

Odessa grabbed another muffin and sprinkled it with powdered pumpkin. "Should we go searching for it?"

"Nope. I want nothing to do with unstable gems." I stretched out my fingers. "I'm still figuring out how to control my own powers."

"Yeah, what's that all about? How come you've got this insanely intense ability to control the weather all of a sudden?" Odessa said. "Have you always had it?"

I bit my lip. "Most likely. Are my parents around?"

"They were, but they've gone out. And your mom seemed tense. I asked her several times if there was anything I could do to help, but she was barely talking to anyone. She even turned down my chocolate chip pancakes, so she must be feeling bad."

"I found out something from my mom when she followed me from the hospital. It's the reason I have these abilities and why I'm no good in the kitchen."

"It's not that you're no good at baking," Odessa said. "It's just your food can be unpredictable."

"That's a nice way of saying my baking magic has always sucked. And there's a good reason for that." I took in a deep breath. The news would get out soon enough, so I didn't feel bad about sharing this secret with Odessa and Cole. "It turns out, my mom had an affair. I was the result."

Odessa's mouth opened. Her forehead wrinkled, and then she nodded. "How do you feel about that?"

"Weird. Mom kept apologizing and saying she wanted to make it up to me, but I don't know if she can. I understand my parents had problems early in their marriage and she made a mistake, but I wish she'd told me sooner. I'd have never gone through all of this, thinking there was something wrong with me. I was so certain I was broken."

"I always knew you weren't," Cole said. "And your power has always felt intriguing to me. It seems like it was hiding, just desperate to come out."

"And now we know why. I was forcing out the wrong magic. And I think I caused all the strange weather around here. Every time I got tangled up in a murder or a mystery in the village, my emotions got the better of me. I created those tornadoes and all the snow."

"You also got rid of the snow," Odessa said. "It was gone within a couple of hours. It shows you can do good with your weather magic."

"And with a little practice, you'll easily control your powers," Cole said.

"Storm will help you with that." Odessa licked caramel sauce off her fingers. "Although her magic always runs cold, and I think you're going to be blazing hot. You'll perfectly complement each other."

"Are Indigo and Storm mad at me for running out of the hospital?"

"No one is mad at you. Sure, we were worried when the nurse said you leaped out the window without being discharged, but there were a lot of us there, and we were asking questions and putting pressure on you. I'd have been tempted to run, too."

"I didn't want to shut you out. None of you." I caught hold of Cole's hand. "I just never wanted to reveal I had a problem."

"It's kind of what friends are there for," Odessa said, "and your delicious werewolf fiancé. What's the point of having us around if we're only here to enjoy the good times? We can help you with the tough stuff, too. That's what real friendship is all about."

I smiled at her, my heart warm with love for my awesome friend. "Thanks. I don't deserve such understanding."

"Oh, don't get me wrong, you have a lot of making up to do. I was thinking I could use your weather magic to help with collecting the pumpkins. Could you handle that? Imagine how awesome it would be if you scooped up the pumpkins in an enormous gust of wind and delivered them to the barn. It would make my job so much easier."

"I might have to practice doing that, but I'm happy to give it a go."

"And you could send tornadoes after some of my pesky scarecrows when they're not behaving."

"Whatever you need. I'm here for you."

"And we're here for you," Cole said.

The main door to the farmhouse opened, and a few seconds later, Indigo and Olympus walked in.

"You're awake." Indigo strode over and hugged me. "Are you ready to talk?"

"I've been filling Odessa in on most of the big stuff."

"Let's not grill her too much," Odessa said. "Luna will only make it snow again if she gets stressed or blow my beautiful farmhouse away with a magic tornado."

"I promise, I'll get a handle on the whole snow thing and the problem tornados. Just take it easy on me if I send a few flurries your way now and again."

"You'd better get a handle on that snow. I don't want to get chilblains." Indigo pulled up a chair, and Olympus sat next to her, a frown on his face.

"Is everything going okay with Alaric and Torin's murder investigations?" I asked him.

Olympus's scowl remained in place. "Reuben isn't talking. He went from saying he was innocent to silence. And Devlin is now having doubts about his guilt, which isn't making this any easier."

I set down my coffee mug. "Who else could it be? Alaric is dead, that frog poisoned Torin, and Elsa works with the Magic Council. That only leaves Reuben. He must have done it."

"That's where the logic leads us, but he's insisting it wasn't him. And he's got Elsa supporting him, too. She showed up a couple of hours ago and has already arranged legal counsel for Reuben. She knows some influential people in the Magic Council, and she's making things difficult for Devlin."

I groaned. "And of course, he's buckling under the pressure."

"You got it. The trouble is, we've searched all of Reuben's things, and there's no evidence he ever found the gem or any of them did." Olympus nodded thanks as Odessa passed him a coffee and a muffin. "With no physical proof he killed Alaric and Torin, we might have to let him go."

"That means he'll get away with a double murder."

"We'll keep looking and asking questions, hoping he slips up, but it's not certain he'll be charged with anything."

I pushed away from the table. "There must be something we can do. I don't suppose Devlin will let me talk to him?"

"Not a chance. And Devlin's just been summoned by the Magic Council to explain how he let a poisonous frog into a secure cell. Stay away from Devlin. He's biting everyone's head off as he flaps around looking for a way out."

"Has Devlin spoken to Killian again?" I said. "He was always unloading equipment and taking the treasure hunters different places. Maybe he saw something odd. He could have seen Reuben fighting with Torin or Alaric. That could be useful."

"Devlin is willing to try anything, but his focus is on questioning Reuben then dealing with his unhappy boss and keeping his new promotion. It's best you don't disturb him," Olympus said.

"He'll bite your head off if you do," Indigo said. "Stay here with us. We have things to talk about."

"We do, but I'm going to drop by and see Killian first. I can ask him about Reuben while I'm there. And I've been meaning to see if there are any volunteering opportunities at the animal sanctuary he's involved with. It could be a great new hobby now I'm no longer baking."

"What will you do for a job if you don't bake anymore?" Indigo said.

"I'm working on it. But I'm definitely staying here." I smiled at Cole. "I have no plans to go anywhere and lots of reasons to stay."

"Hmmm. We'll be here when you're ready to fill in the rest of the missing pieces." Indigo didn't look thrilled I was leaving, but I couldn't relax until we got proof of Reuben's guilt.

"I promise, we'll talk real soon." After a quick goodbye to everyone, I left the farmhouse with Earl and headed to the edge of Witch Haven.

Killian lived in a small hut in a quiet part of the village on a piece of disused farmland. There was a dirt track leading up to his hut and three large barns set out the back.

As I walked along the path, a three-legged floppy eared gray rabbit loped out of the bushes in front of me. It was followed by a small ginger cat with only one eye and a tailless brown house rat.

"Luna!" Killian shielded his eyes with his hand as he stood outside a barn.

Earl slid off my shoulders and stalked the animals that had run past.

"No eating them," I whispered. "Be on your best behavior."

He didn't respond as his ears lowered and he sank to his belly.

I raised a hand as I walked over to Killian. "Hey. I hope you don't mind me dropping by unannounced."

"No, of course not. I'm just surprised to see you out here. Not many people come this way. There's not much here other than tumbleweed, me, and orphan animals."

"I wanted to ask you about Reuben. He still hasn't confessed to the murders, and I wondered if you saw anything odd when you were at their camp, anything that made you suspicious about him. The Magic Council is struggling to get evidence, and I'd hate it if he got away."

"I'm not finished with you!" Rainbow Dazzlewillow shot out of the barn, her wings quivering.

Killian's normally cheerful expression soured. "Hang on a minute, Luna." He turned to Rainbow. "I appreciate the visit, but I'm not interested in helping."

Rainbow glanced at me and then focused back on Killian. "You must. You could be the face of one of our campaigns. You're not unattractive when you tidy yourself up. Plenty of women like the scruffy look."

"Thanks for the compliment, but it's still a no."

"What's going on?" I said.

Rainbow hissed out an angry breath. "I've offered Killian the opportunity of a lifetime, and he's turned me down."

"I can't handle any more jobs. I've got enough on my hands with the animal sanctuary and my current bookings."

"By the looks of this place, you need to handle them." Rainbow's nose wrinkled as she fluttered around. "If you invest some capital here, you could have a base camp for future treasure hunts. You could charge for the accommodation."

"I get by just fine. And don't insult my home."

"I've projected we can increase tourism by twenty-two percent if we do an intensive promotion focusing on the treasure hunts. You'll get a cut of that money. And I might be able to convince the photographer to pay you if you take part in the photoshoot."

"It's not a bad idea," I said. "And you could spend the extra money on the animals you rescue."

"Exactly. I see no problems with this." Rainbow gave me an approving nod. "It's a sound moneymaking venture. And all the local businesses will benefit, including Fandango's when it finally reopens. Where have you gotten with setting up a temporary store, Luna?"

I stepped back under her intense glare. "Um, I kind of looked into it. Uncle Albert likes the idea of using the store next door, but he's still recovering. And I'm no longer baking, so nothing will happen for a few weeks."

"No longer baking? You must!"

"No, I don't. Not anymore. I have new magic. Well, not new, but different. Don't worry, you'll get your bakery back, and it'll be twice as good as it was." Especially if I was no longer doing anything with the food.

"Humph! We'll see about that." Rainbow fluttered around and lasered her glare back on Killian. "I'll send over the contract about expanding the treasure hunting."

He shook his head. "You're wasting your time. I'm not doing it."

"I'll be back tomorrow when you've seen sense." Rainbow fluttered away, muttering shrill fairy curses for anyone to hear.

Killian turned away from me, his hands clenched as he heaved in deep breaths.

"Don't you think you can handle the extra work?" I said.

"Yeah, something like that." He let out a sigh and turned back to face me. "Sorry, I didn't mean to get angry, but Rainbow pushes my buttons. She never gives up when she wants something. You were saying something about Reuben?"

I nodded. "The Magic Council needs proof he killed Alaric and Torin. Without it, they might have to let him go."

Killian scrubbed his chin. "I wish I could help, but I wasn't around their camp that much. I'd pick them up, drop them off, and deal with their equipment, but that was about it."

That wasn't the information I wanted. "Do you think Reuben could be the killer? Did he do anything to make you wary of him?"

He lifted his hands. "Maybe. I don't know. He was a bit of a slob and would leave litter around. Elsa always nagged him about it."

"Going from dropping litter to a crazed killer is a stretch, but it must be him." A strange low moaning sound reached my ears, and I tilted my head. "What's that?"

"It's a baby abath. He was orphaned, so I took him in."

"He sounds in pain."

"No, it's the sound he makes when he wants attention or he gets scared. He's a cute little guy if you want to meet him. He hates being left alone for long, so I take him everywhere with me."

"Sure. And I wanted to ask you about volunteering at the animal sanctuary, too. I'd love to help since I've got more free time."

"We always welcome extra hands. This way. You can have a look and see what you might be getting into. I keep some rescues here while they're recuperating. They like the quiet." Killian led me into one of the barns. There were a dozen stalls inside, and most of them were filled with hay and water buckets. He led me to the end stall, where a cute abath stood. He was a beautiful pearly gray color with large black eyes and a tiny horn nub in the middle of his head.

He wobbled over on too long spindly legs the second he saw Killian and made that eerie honking noise again. His front left leg was wrapped in a blue bandage.

Killian petted the abath's head. "He thinks I'm his mom. I've been hand rearing him ever since I found him alone in the forest. The plan is to get him independent and see how he manages on his own."

"I'm surprised you can let him go when he gets big enough to look after himself. I'd get too attached to the animals."

"It's tough. And I often end up keeping a few around here. I can never refuse them, especially when the sanctuary is full."

I gently petted the creature. "It must be so rewarding doing this."

"It sure is. Although the sanctuary is always in need of more money. I donate what I can from my treasure hunts."

"Maybe you should take Rainbow up on her offer. It would help."

He shook his head. "Not a chance."

Earl bounded into the barn. He leaped on my shoulder and stuck his damp nose right in my ear. "You have to see something I found."

"You didn't chase any of the animals, did you?"

"Only for a few minutes. They're fast. They all got away." Earl glanced at Killian.

"I need to feed this little guy," Killian said. "Take a look around the other barns if you like. Just stay out of the one at the end. Some of the animals in there are skittish, and you don't want to scare them."

"Sure. Thanks." I hurried out with Earl. "What did you find?"

"It's in that end barn."

I groaned. "The one Killian told us not to go in?"

"Yep. And there's a good reason he told us not to poke around in there. Hurry!"

I dashed to the barn, making sure Killian wasn't watching where we were going, then eased open the door and slipped inside. It was gloomy as I shut the door, but I followed Earl's directions to the back of the barn.

"Keep going right to the end. It's in the back in the right-hand corner," he hiss-whispered.

When I got there, my mouth fell open. There was a tank with three of the rare purple devil frogs inside.

"Killian has a collection of those poisonous little critters," Earl said. "Why is he keeping lethal weapons in his barn? A weapon used to kill Torin."

I couldn't believe what I was seeing. "He... he can't be the killer. Killian is a pacifist. And he loves animals. I don't even think he eats meat. He's a gentle soul."

"If he's such a good guy, why has he got a stash of deadly weapons in a glass tank?"

I heard the faint ghostly honk moan of the abath Killian was feeding. "When Elsa was first interviewed after Alaric's murder, she mentioned hearing a strange ghostly groan. Do you think Killian had the abath with him that night? He couldn't leave it behind because it was too vulnerable, so he stashed the baby in the truck while he crept to the camp."

"It looks young. Most babies panic if they get left on their own."

"And it must need bottle feeding every few hours. Killian couldn't take the risk of leaving the abath." I didn't want it to be him, but with that spooky noise echoing around me and his collection of poisonous devil frogs in front of me, it was suddenly obvious.

I dashed to the door and pulled it open. Killian was standing outside.

Chapter 18

"Oh! Sorry for poking around in here. I couldn't resist taking a peek everywhere." I eased the door shut behind me, taking a breath to calm my racing heart.

Killian blocked me from moving away from the barn. "I hope you didn't disturb any of the animals. Some of them are sensitive to light."

"No, and I only took a really quick look. I didn't even get to the end stall." I inched away, my fingers wrapped around Earl's tail. "I'll be going now."

He sighed. "You saw the frogs, didn't you?"

I tried to look as innocent as possible. "Frogs?"

Killian ran a hand down his face. "Yeah, you saw them. I'm transferring them to a herpetologist soon for further study and protection. I found a small colony of them in the woods."

"Well, that's great. Good luck with that. I'll get out of your way. You must be busy."

He stepped into my path. "I thought you wanted to know about volunteering at the sanctuary."

"Of course! But I've just remembered I need to be somewhere. Cole's expecting me. He'll come looking for me if I don't meet him. You know how possessive these werewolves can be."

Killian grabbed my arm. "Then I need to make this quick. I'm really sorry, Luna, but you can't leave. Neither of you can."

I struggled in his strong grip. "Why not? You can't keep me here."

"I'm going to have to." He sighed. "What a mess. I really like you, but you're always poking around and asking too many questions."

"Only because I want Alaric and Torin's murderer caught," I said.

The abath made that strange ghostly moan honk again.

Killian raked a hand through his hair. "If only you hadn't come here, I could have figured something out."

"Figured out a way to frame Reuben, you mean?"

He didn't say anything, but a muscle in his jaw clenched.

"It was you, wasn't it? The abath call was what Elsa heard the night of Alaric's murder. You had to bring him with you in your truck."

"You don't know what you're talking about. Please stop. You're only making things worse for yourself."

I shook my head, even though my heart beat so fast I felt faint. "And the poisonous purple devil frogs. What did you do, slip one into Torin's pocket just before he got taken into the cell?"

"You can't prove that. Torin was just unlucky."

"You said the frogs were rare. One wouldn't have followed him into that cell. You planted it when you grabbed him to stop the fight with Devlin. Did you have the frogs in your truck?"

His fingers flexed around my arm. "I'm... protecting the innocent. I'm not doing anything wrong."

"I understand you're protective of the woods and the animals who live there." I hoped to appeal to his gentle nature. "It must get annoying when treasure hunters show up and mess with that sanctuary. They make fires, leave litter, and stamp around."

"Some of them have no respect for the place. They're only interested in what they can gain. And I couldn't believe it when Torin used explosives to clear the tunnels. He killed animals! But he didn't care. He didn't even notice when I pointed out the nest of pale warblers that got knocked from the tree."

"So you decided to kill him?"

"I never said I killed him."

"I understand why you want to protect the animals. I almost killed Reuben because I thought he'd poisoned Earl."

"And all the time it was you," Earl hissed.

Killian looked away, his cheeks flushing.

"You're passionate about animal welfare, but killing people is wrong," I said.

"But ruining a precious woodland and trampling all over the animals' homes is okay?"

"No, of course not. It all needs careful management." I tried to get my arm free, but Killian refused to release me. "And that's why you were resistant to Rainbow's idea about expanding the business. It would have meant more animals being hounded out of their homes or hurt."

"I can't let that happen." He scowled at the ground. "Rainbow doesn't understand. All she can see is the profit, not the damage expanding tourism would do. I can handle a few groups going in now and again. I always ask them to be careful, and most of them listen, but there are a few, like the last group, who thought they knew better. They were planning to excavate without any thought of the damage to the environment."

"You could have asked them to stop. I didn't know Alaric well, but he seemed like a reasonable guy. He would have understood the need to be careful."

"I did. But he was as obsessed as the rest of them. He found part of an old map that suggested the gem was underground. All he wanted was to find that gem. Alaric didn't care what he destroyed to achieve his goal."

I nodded, hoping my expression was one of understanding. "And if that happened, it would have created a floodgate of damaging tourism. Everyone would visit the woods to see the spot and maybe look for their own treasure."

"All encouraged by that selfish PR fairy. I spoke to Alaric. I even tried to take the map from him. I did everything to convince him not to keep on with the treasure hunt, but he said he had to."

"Did you mean to kill him?" I said.

A tortured sigh slid from his lips. "Luna, I'm not a bad person, but Alaric left me with no choice. He refused to listen to reason. I couldn't trust him."

"So you stabbed him."

He swallowed. "I didn't go to his tent that night with a plan to kill him. I figured Alaric was a smart guy and would understand me. I knew, if I got through to him, the others would follow. They'd have turned the visit into a fun camping trip and left with a few wild stories to tell their friends."

"Did you take the knife into his tent?"

"No! Alaric had it in there when I arrived. I got so angry when he didn't listen to me. And I saw it lying there after he told me to leave. It was in my hand before I realized what I was doing. I only meant to threaten him, but then... he lunged at me. I didn't even think about it."

"But you did sneak back to the camp that night and made sure no one saw you."

"No one else needed to be involved in our discussion. I figured, if I got Alaric on his own and convinced him to do the right thing, then he'd make the rest of the treasure hunters leave."

Earl stuck his nose in my ear. "He's never going to let us go now he's just confessed."

I knew that was true. Killian almost seemed relieved he was confessing to the murders, but it left us in a difficult situation. "What about Torin? Did you try to convince him, too?"

He made a noise of exasperation. "That would have been a waste of time. Torin didn't care what damage he caused, so long as he got that gem. I learned he was planning to sell a story of their cursed trip to a national newspaper. He'd already gotten everything arranged and had done a deal with them. It would sensationalize the mysterious gem. Everyone would have visited to find it. These animals deserve so much better."

"So you poisoned him with one of your frogs?"

"It wasn't planned. It was a coincidence I had the purple devil frogs in the back of my truck. And I really was only driving past when I saw Torin's fight with Devlin. I pulled over when I heard them. Torin was yelling that he planned to tell everyone about this place. I couldn't let him get away with it. I've always got protective gloves I use to handle dangerous animals, so I slipped one on and grabbed a frog."

"Didn't Torin or Devlin see what you were doing?"

"Devlin was too busy worrying about his broken nose, and Torin was too angry to focus on me. It wasn't hard to catch hold of him and slip the frog into his pocket. I made it look like I was trying to help him and stop him from getting in more trouble with the Magic Council. Then I had to hope the frog would do its job." Killian glanced at Earl. "I'm sorry you got injured. I'm glad you're okay."

"I'll be even better if you let us go," Earl said.

Killian shook his head. "I wish I could. What I did was for the greater good. The woods need protecting, and I'm determined to do that. And that means I must silence both of you. The animals are more important than a single witch and her familiar."

"You won't kill us, Killian. You only murdered Alaric and Torin to protect something you loved. I understand that. I've never hurt your woods. And I love animals as much as you do. You need to come clean, though. An innocent man is being held on a double murder charge."

"Reuben's not innocent. He was going along with the plans to blow up parts of the woods and kill animals."

"But he didn't deliberately murder two people."

"What he had planned was just as bad. I had to stop it." Anger glinted in Killian's eyes. "I'm done taking people into the woods. I only do it so I can keep an eye on them and make sure they don't cause too much harm. I've already submitted a protection order on the place. It'll stop anyone from going there without the right permits."

"That's good. But I still can't let you get away with this."

"You don't have a choice." Killian moved so fast he was a blur. He grabbed Earl by the scruff, opened the barn door, and tossed him inside before slamming it shut.

I raced to the door to free Earl, who was hissing and snarling on the other side.

Killian shoved me away. "I'll make it quick. There'll be little pain."

"You're not thinking straight. If I go missing, people will notice. They'll look for me. And my friends know I was visiting you. You won't get away with this."

Magic sparked on Killian's fingers. "You're trespassing. I'll claim I killed you in self-defense. And your new magic could be unstable. It won't take much to convince that idiot Devlin you attacked me and I had to defend myself. I know he doesn't like you."

"Earl will tell the truth about what happened here." I stayed close to the barn so I could grab any chance to free my familiar.

"That cat is useless. I've seen him staggering about the village, high as a kite. He's not a reliable witness. And if he survives your death, I'll simply relocate him. He'll forget you. He'll probably be glad to have a fresh start."

I snarled at Killian. "No, he won't. He's the perfect familiar, just like I'm a good witch. You're not going to hurt him." My palms were sweating, my pulse racing, and my spine shook, but I wasn't running from this fight.

Power tingled through me, mingling with my terror and anger. I shoved out the spell that felt desperate to emerge. It poured out of me in a hot, jagged bolt of lightning.

Killian threw himself out of the way, rolling to his feet and slamming a sparking spell my way.

I tossed it aside and refocused. This weather magic was new to me, so I wasn't sure what I could do. And my emotions influenced it, and they were a mess. This fight could get chaotic.

A tingling spread down my arms as a rumble of thunder shook the clouds. "Give up, Killian. It doesn't have to end this way. None of us need to get hurt."

His gaze lifted to the rolling black clouds pouring in from all directions. "I won't stop this fight to protect the woods. They're too important to me."

I attempted another lightning bolt, but the magic scattered across the ground and fizzled in the dirt.

Killian lunged at me, his hands hot with magic as they made contact.

A scream flew from my lips. I grabbed his arms and clung to him to stop him from throttling me.

He hissed and yanked his arm away but not before I saw a perfect burn handprint on his arm.

I backed away. "How did you get that burn? Alaric had fire magic. Did he fight back when you stabbed him?"

"Never mind how I got it. Just give up. Stop fighting me. This is the right thing to do."

"Being murdered by you will never be the right thing for me."

Another weather spell simmered inside me, but my heartbeat was frantic, and my breath rasped out of me. I didn't have control over this intense spell. And I couldn't hear Earl anymore. Where was he? Was he hurt?

The magic flickered from my fingers, but my lack of focus sent it shooting in all directions, including back into my chest, whipping my breath from me and making my throat tighten.

"You're a failed witch. This ends now." Killian had me backed against the wall, and I had nowhere to go.

He grabbed a pitchfork and whacked the flat of his hand against it, making the metal glow. "Sorry, Luna. I like you, but I'll do whatever I have to in order to keep people away from the woods."

A screeching, hissing black ball of fury blasted around the side of the barn and leaped on Killian's head.

Chapter 19

"Get him off me! He's trying to gouge out my eyes." Killian's shriek was high-pitched as he stumbled back and landed in the dirt.

"I thought you loved all animals." I stared at Earl as he clung to Killian's face, his claws buried deep in his cheeks and his teeth dug in his forehead. Tiny lightning sparks blasted out of my amazing familiar as he attacked.

Killian yelped and flailed his arms.

"Don't let him go!" Magic pulsed out of me in rapid waves in time with my racing heartbeat. Wind swirled around Killian and Earl, and Killian was lifted off his feet by the tornado I wrapped around him.

"Confess what you did to the Magic Council, and they might be lenient. You were protecting what you loved. They'll understand." I doubted they would, but I wasn't prepared to let Killian go until he agreed to reveal what he'd done.

"Get Earl off me. He's going for my eyes. I'll be blinded."

"I can't do that. And he'll keep going for your eyes until you tell the truth." I intensified my magic, and Killian rose higher until he was ten feet off the ground.

The air around me heated, and a second later, Devlin and two members of the Magic Council appeared.

His eyes narrowed and then he shook his head. "I should have known you'd be in the middle of something dubious like this. What are you doing to Killian? And is that Earl on his head?"

I didn't let my attention drift from Killian. "Dubious? How did you know I was here?"

"I had a report of unnatural weather taking place in this location. We've been monitoring the unusual weather situation since it began and get alerts when something flares. I'm involved in the committee to ensure whoever is doing it is stopped."

"Of course you are. Who doesn't love a committee?" I raised my hands, and Killian shrieked again. "Well, this weather is mine, and I'm seventy percent sure I'm in control of it. Although you might want to stand back in case you get caught up in the tornado."

"Put Killian back on the ground."

"I will. But you need to know he's your killer."

Devlin glared at Killian and then me. Hope glittered in his eyes. "Not Reuben? Tell me more."

It was a positive start. At least Devlin wasn't threatening to arrest me. "Killian murdered Alaric because he wouldn't stop looking for the gem."

"Killian wanted the gem for himself?"

"No. He doesn't care about the gem. He didn't want anyone damaging the woods trying to find it."

"And Torin? Why kill him?"

"To stop him from selling a story to a national newspaper about how incredible the woods are."

"Why does that matter?"

"Killian's a conservationist. He was worried the woods were being damaged. The extra tourism generated from that story would have only made things worse."

Devlin took in a slow, deep breath but didn't say anything.

This could go one of two ways. I could be arrested and charged with assaulting Killian, or Devlin would finally believe something I told him.

His gaze flicked back to Killian, who was still battling the tornado and Earl. "It does explain why Reuben is so certain he didn't do it. And... we've not found any evidence to implicate him."

My eyebrows shot up. "You think I'm telling the truth?"

"I knew something wasn't right about Reuben's arrest. And Elsa is insisting we release him as soon as possible. She's being stubborn about it."

"I was in agreement with you. I thought it was Reuben, too. But Killian confessed to me. He did it to protect the woods. Ask him."

"You need to let him down and get Earl off his face before I can do that." Devlin gestured his colleagues to surround Killian. "Watch him. Make sure he doesn't get away."

I concentrated on drawing in my magic, and then slowly lowered Killian to the ground. "You can let go, Earl. He's not going anywhere."

Earl kicked off Killian's face in an impressive ninja move, leaving behind deep gouge marks. He was still sparking with lightning as he reached my side, a smug look on his furry face. "No one scruffs me and gets away with it."

I went to give him a well done pet, but he growled, his fur fluffed out and shimmering.

"Sorry. I'm still getting used to all this power. I'm over-excited." Earl shook himself, and his fur flattened.

Devlin moved closer to Killian, who was huddled in the dirt, his chest heaving. "Is there truth to what Luna just told me? You killed Alaric and Torin?"

"Arrest her! She's insane. She probably killed those guys." Killian glared at me as he gingerly touched his wounded face. "And Luna attacked me for no reason."

"Don't believe him." Killian wasn't pinning this on me, but he might plant doubt in Devlin's easily manipulated mind and give himself a chance to escape.

"You know me, Devlin. I'm not a murderer," Killian said.

"You keep going like that, and I'll use my tornado on you again." I lifted my hands.

Devlin shook his head at me. "We have things under control. And Killian is a good guy. I'm certain he'll be willing to answer a few questions."

"If it clears me of Luna's accusations, I'm happy to." Killian staggered to his feet.

"You do plenty of excellent work in Witch Haven," Devlin said. "We all appreciate your help with the woods and making sure the animals have homes. My great aunt adopted a yellow-tailed parrot from you years ago. The bird makes her very happy."

He grinned, flicked his gaze at me, and stood taller. "I'm always glad to help."

"I remember how passionate you were about conservation back then." Devlin straightened his hat. "And I've also heard about your work to have the woods re-classified."

"Err... sure. They need to be. People take advantage. No one else is doing anything about it. The landowner doesn't care. He's only interested in making money."

"And that's wrong?"

"Yeah, it is. Nature deserves better."

"Is that a confession?" Devlin said.

Killian jerked back. "No, it's not. I thought we were on the same page."

"Take a look in the barn," I said. "There are more purple devil frogs in there. Killian said they're rare, so it's unlikely he's keeping them as pets. He had them in his truck and slipped one into Torin's pocket just before you took him away after he punched you."

Devlin's hand went to his nose. "I wondered why you got involved in that altercation. Was it so you could plant the murder weapon on Torin?"

Killian huffed out a breath. "You seriously believe her?" He jabbed a finger at me.

"And ask Elsa about the strange noise she heard on the night Alaric was murdered. She'll identify it as the baby abath Killian has in his barn. He had it with him the night he snuck into Alaric's tent and killed him. It was in the truck."

Killian's nostrils flared, and his hands flexed into fists. "That could have been another abath. All babies look alike."

"One with a blue bandage on his front leg? Elsa said she saw something on its leg that night."

Killian heaved out a sigh. "Maybe. It was dark. She could have made a mistake."

"The abath got out of your truck, didn't he? You had to see Alaric and couldn't leave the infant on his own. He snuck out and almost gave you away when he alarm called."

"Are you going to get him to testify against me?" Killian said.

"We'll take it from here." Devlin sent his colleagues over to secure Killian. He turned to me. "How did you know it was him?"

"I didn't. Not until I looked around his barn and saw the tank of frogs and the injured abath and heard his cries. Then everything fell into place."

Devlin scrubbed the back of his neck. "Now I have something positive to report to the Magic Council. My superiors have been demanding a resolution to this investigation. And I haven't been able to get Rainbow Dazzlewillow off my back. She wants these murders solved so her tourism figures aren't impacted."

Killian groaned. "It's not right. None of that should be happening."

"Take him away," Devlin said to his colleagues. He nodded at me, and they all vanished.

I did a slow circle as I looked around Killian's home. It sounded like all the barns had animals in them, and from the noise they were making, they'd picked up on the fighting and were anxious.

"Shall we get out of here?" Earl said. "After finding the killer, we should treat ourselves."

"You mean, me buying you more catnip?"

"Nope. I meant what I said. I don't need that stuff anymore. Now I have my real power, I can be a proper familiar to you." He looked up at me. "If you'll let me."

I scooped him up, not minding the tiny electric shocks he gave me. My heart was full of love for this perfect furball. "And all this time, I never realized what an amazing team we could be."

"I thought you sucked, too. And you used to bug the heck out of me, always forcing yourself to spend time in the kitchen making those revolting cakes."

"Hey! They weren't all revolting."

"True. Some of them were just inferior gloopy disasters." He booped his nose on my cheek. "It never did us any good to force something we weren't meant to do."

"Not anymore. No more cakes for us. We have a new adventure to begin." I walked over and pulled open one of the barn doors. There were twelve stalls inside, all full of orphaned animals. "So, what shall we do with this lot?"

***

"If you put those last few animals in the end storage shed, there's room in there." I swiped a hand across my sweaty forehead and smiled as Ridley, Gloria, and Fay herded the animals into the shed.

After discovering Killian was looking after thirty sick or orphaned animals, there was no way I could abandon them. So after some quick thinking and pulling a couple of late nights, I'd worked with my farmhouse tenants, no longer my magical harem, and my other friends to erect temporary homes for the animals.

I had the space at my farmhouse, and now Gloria, Fay, and Ridley were free to use their magic how they liked, they'd have more time on their hands to be animal guardians.

Cole wrapped his arms around me from behind and rested his chin on the top of my head. "This lot will keep you busy."

"Which is just what I need." I rested back against him. Cole had been happy to help move the animals and set up their homes as soon as he learned what I was doing. We worked well together. We'd had the occasional bicker, but we were still figuring out how to be a couple. And an engaged couple at that. It was one lie I was happy to turn into the truth. I was a blissfully engaged witch. I still had to pinch myself.

Indigo and Olympus walked over, coming from the direction of the village. Devlin was also with them.

"We thought you might need a hand," Indigo said. "I brought some muscle. Well, Olympus. But you look like you're almost done."

"Everyone still needs feeding. There's plenty to do." I looked at Devlin. "How's everything going with Killian?"

His eyes narrowed a fraction, but then he nodded. "He was hard work, but I kept pressing him. I've been on an advanced interview techniques course, so I know how to deal with difficult suspects."

Indigo stifled a laugh behind her hand. "Sounds intense."

Olympus nudged her. "It is. I've been on it too."

Devlin's lips pursed, but he carried on. "It turns out, Killian's been trying to buy the land from Bart Hogarth for years without success. Some of his letters got threatening when Bart kept turning him down. Killian wanted to turn it into a protected site and prevent anyone from going on it without his permission. Keeping that land and the animals safe meant more to him than anything else."

"Did he confess to the killings?" I asked.

"Not straight away. But with the threatening letters sent to Bart, Elsa confirming the sighting of the injured abath in the woods, and a court order to view Killian's juvenile record, he gave in."

"He has a juvenile record?"

Olympus nodded. "He was an eco-terrorist. He did some shady things when he was a teenager. People got injured when he set up a magical ward around a section of parkland. He was lucky not to go to jail."

"But he will now," Devlin said.

"I almost wish it wasn't him," I said. "Killian was trying to do the right thing. He just went about it terribly."

"Murder is never right," Devlin said.

Everyone nodded sagely, and an awkward silence descended.

I clapped my hands together. "Devlin, do you want to lend a hand with the animals? There are some cute ones here. Some of them are also looking to be adopted if you have a home to give them. Didn't you say your great aunt has parrots? We have several birds. You might like one of those."

"That awful parrot is a beast. It always tries to peck me when I visit. I don't think it likes me." Devlin pulled out a pair of thick gloves from his pocket and removed his hat. "But I can help with the animals. What do you want me to do?"

I hid my surprise as I led him to a barn and showed him the food and water the animals needed.

He touched my elbow just before I left him to get to work. "Thank you for your assistance in solving these murders. I was being pressured into finding evidence against Reuben, and I wasn't sure what to do. My career was under threat. It's... it's all I have. And it's important to me."

"Are you sure you don't want to adopt an animal? It would give you something else to enjoy."

His forehead wrinkled. "I'll think about it. Maybe something small wouldn't be so bad."

I couldn't leave him when he seemed so uncertain, clutching his hat as he looked around like a lost puppy. "Devlin, I never wanted to be your enemy. I know we don't always see eye to eye, but I was making sure the bad guys didn't get away with it. I don't want you to consider me a bad person."

His gaze met mine, and he nodded. "There was a time when I thought you were. I was wrong about that. I've closed the case on the complaints about the bakery. My understanding is you weren't aware of your abilities, so you had no way of knowing you were misusing your power."

That was a lot more than I'd expected to hear from him. Since he was holding out the olive branch, I'd grab it. "I appreciate that. Thank you. And, I promise, no more baking. And I'll be careful with my weather magic until it's fully under my control. I'm already improving."

"Make sure you do. And... there was a warlock found encased in ice by the hospital."

I stiffened. "Was there?"

"We got an anonymous tip about him. It was Bram Vexx. The person who robbed the bakery." Devlin waited for me to speak, but I was saying nothing. "Did you have anything to do with catching him?"

"Will I get in trouble if I say yes?"

He pinched the bridge of his nose. "Bram admitted to the robbery. He said he was forced to put magic explosives in the bakery, and he's pointing the finger at his boss. He's asked for immunity against prosecution if he reveals what his boss has been doing. If we give him a deal, he'll get relocated, a new identity, and a chance at a new life."

I tilted my head. "You're interested in going after Sylvester Mahoney?"

A frown crossed his face. "I don't even want to know how you know that name. But yes, we've been after Sylvester for years. We've never had a better opportunity to take him down."

"Then do it! Give Bram a second chance and take down Sylvester. They're both shady guys, though, so don't be too lenient with Bram."

"And you know that how?"

"Um... it's best you don't know. But it'll impress the Magic Council if you get Sylvester off the street."

Devlin still didn't look all that happy. "True. I'll file the paperwork for Bram's immunity later."

"It seems everyone got what they deserved." I grinned at him. "Now, all we need to do is find you something cute and fluffy to love, and everything will be perfect."

He nodded and then got to work on feeding the animals.

I smiled as I left Devlin to it. I'd made a new friend, or at least I no longer had an enemy after me. It was a great start.

I headed back outside to find my parents had arrived with Odessa and Storm. Odessa was unpacking a hamper of treats on a long table she'd set up.

She smiled when she saw me. "I figured all the hard workers would appreciate a break."

"This all looks great." My stomach growled as I looked at the delicious treats. I glanced at my parents. They were standing apart from each other, both looking miserable. "I thought you were bringing Uncle Albert with you."

A smile crossed my mom's face. "He's right behind us. He's bringing a date."

"He is?" My gaze shifted along the road, and I laughed. Uncle Albert had Tabitha with him.

"She seems nice," my mom said. "Albert invited her over for tea and cakes yesterday, and she didn't leave until almost midnight."

"I'm happy for him. He deserves someone special in his life."

Mom glanced at my dad. "We all do. Can you spare us a moment? We've barely had time to speak since you've been working to find homes for these animals."

I mustered a smile, not wanting to tackle this topic. "I'm keeping them all here for now. I figured I'd set up a sanctuary. I have the room and all the help I need." I gestured to Ridley as he chased down a fluffy escapee with horns.

"That all sounds interesting," Dad said. "Please, I would like to talk to you. I have things I need to say."

I was about to protest, but I'd put this off for too long. And I had been avoiding my parents. "Sure. Why don't we go under the shade of that tree? We'll get sunburned if we stay out here too long."

Ever since I'd gotten control of my magic, I figured I might as well make the most of it. It was a warm pleasant day, and there was a light breeze in the air. There was no sign of snow, tornadoes, or lightning storms. Although, depending on what my dad was about to tell me, that might change.

I walked away from everyone else with my parents. I waited for them to start. There was still a lot of forgiving to do.

"I wanted to talk to you about your wedding to Cole," my dad said.

Mom sighed. "We wanted to talk to you about it. But not right away. There's something much more important to deal with."

"You're still together?" I said.

Mom lowered her gaze. "We're working on it. We have a lot to figure out, but your father knows everything."

I glanced at my dad, my stomach twisted in knots and my eyes hazing with tears. "I understand if you don't want anything to do with me. It must have been a shock when you found out I wasn't your daughter."

"No, it actually wasn't." He reached for my hand, and I grabbed it. "I've always known you were different from the rest of the family. Your power has always had a strange flare to it. And I did wonder if your mother had an indiscretion early in our marriage. Things were strained for some time until you came along."

"You never asked Mom about it?"

"No. It seemed easier. And we both found happiness. We also had you, and I'd never want that to change." His eyes grew glassy, and he blinked several times.

"You must be angry because the truth was hidden for such a long time. I was."

"Yes. But not for long. I was more concerned with the damage we'd done to you. And we're both at fault for that. I should have confronted your mother. We should have helped you. Paid you more attention. That was selfish of us."

I swallowed, my throat tight. "It wasn't always easy, but maybe I should have asked for help. I got great at hiding things. I never wanted to be a problem."

"You would never be a problem." Dad squeezed my hand, and his gaze moved to my mom. "And we're discussing what to do next. Our marriage is based on more than just affection. We're business people first and foremost. To separate would harm our standing in the baking community. We have to consider that."

"You also have to consider your own happiness. Is staying together and going for the top slot in the baking dynasty going to bring you satisfaction?"

They shared an amused smile. There was still a bond between them, even if it was messed up.

"It is. And we don't expect you to understand that. But that doesn't mean we love you any less," my dad said. "Even though you aren't my biological daughter, you are mine. I will always be there to love and support you. And I'll be around more. If I had been when you were younger, I'd have seen things weren't right with your baking magic."

"The same goes for me. I plan to visit much more often," my mom said.

"Um, that's great."

"But..." Mom tilted her head. "You don't want us around?"

"I want you happy. Baking does that. And I know you like seeing me, but tearing you from your passion would make all of us miserable. How about I come visit you more often? You keep telling me there's a huge world out there waiting to be explored. I can do that now. Especially if Uncle Albert gets serious with Tabitha. He won't want me being his third wheel."

"We'd love that." Mom hugged me.

I'd never fully understand my parents' obsession with baking and putting it before anything else, but now I had my natural ability fired up, it made more sense. My weather magic spoke to me in a way I'd never experienced before. It was a part of me, and I couldn't imagine being without it.

"We have a lot to work through." Mom stepped back. "But don't give up on us. We'll try our best. But you must say if we're getting distracted or too pushy. We know we're not the easiest people to be around."

"I'll send a bolt of lightning your way, shall I? That might get your attention when you're elbows deep in your favorite dough mix."

"That it would." Dad wrapped me in a warm hug.

"So, about your wedding," my mom said, "we'd both like to be involved. I've agreed your father can make the cake, providing I make the rest of the food. I was thinking a six course banquet."

I choked out a laugh. "That's generous. And werewolves have big appetites, so I'm sure they'll appreciate it. But just so you know, we're planning on a long engagement."

"More precisely, Luna's planning on a long engagement." Cole strolled over. "I couldn't help but overhear you talking about our wedding. I want to marry this beautiful, talented witch as soon as she'll let me."

"Of course. You must be involved too," my mom said. "And we should arrange to meet your family. We can have a pre-wedding dinner, and everyone can discuss the plans."

Cole wrapped an arm around my waist. "So long as there's food involved, I'm on board. And Luna can have whatever wedding she desires, whenever she desires it."

"I really would like to keep the ceremony simple, but perhaps we can go all out on the food. That way, everyone's happy." I snuggled against Cole.

Mom and Dad nodded their approval.

Uncle Albert and Tabitha arrived, and he made the introductions, his cheeks flushed pink and a smile on his face as he presented his new girlfriend.

We returned to the food table. Gloria, Fay, and Ridley joined us, along with everyone else. We were one huge, messy, multifaceted family, and I couldn't have been happier to be in the middle of it.

Earl snaked around my ankles, and his purr vibrated up my calf. He was looking fatter and sleeker than I'd ever seen him. This weather magic agreed with him.

He caught my eye and winked. I tossed him a piece of bacon pancake to enjoy.

I tipped my head back and enjoyed the sun on my face and the all-encompassing warmth of the amazing friends and family around me. I still had things to learn, and it would take a while to get full control of my new power, but just like the sun blazing overhead, the outlook looked bright.

About Author

K.E. O'Connor (Karen) is a mystery author living in the beautiful British countryside. She loves all things mystery, animals, and cake.

If you want to be part of the Witch Haven crew, practice spells, solve a few murders, spend time with amazing witches and their talking familiars, and get a **free** book, join her weekly newsletter.

Sign up today.

Newsletter:
https://BookHip.com/QKGDWJW
Website:
www.keoconnor.com/writing
Facebook:
www.facebook.com/keoconnorauthor

Also By

Spells and Spooks
Hexes and Haunts
Curses and Corpses
Muffins and Moonlight
Cupcakes and Cauldrons
Pancakes and Potions
Hauntings and High Jinx
Hauntings and Havoc
Hauntings and Hoaxes
The Case of the Screaming Skull
The Case of the Poisoned Pumpkin
The Case of the Cursed Candy
Fire Fang
Silvaria

If you enjoyed

Pancakes and Potions

turn the page to read an extract from the
next Witch Haven mystery. This book features
Odessa Grimsbane as our main witchy sleuth. This
pumpkin-obsessed witch has a haunting secret,
some troublesome scarecrows to deal with, and
murders to solve!

HAUNTINGS AND HIGH JINX
ISBN: 978-1-915378-34-7

Chapter 1

"Those are his footprints. I'd recognize Michael's size thirteen feet anywhere. I accidentally gave him an extra toe on his right foot." I kneeled beside the deep imprint in the mud and placed my hand inside it.

My faithful scarecrow companion, Shamrock, loomed over me. The glow in his eyes helped to illuminate the darkness, but there was still no sign of Michael. We'd been looking for over an hour, and I was trying not to panic.

I stood and brushed dirt off my leggings. "What's gotten into him? This is the fifth time he's escaped."

Shamrock shrugged a huge shoulder as he scanned our surroundings.

I'd given Michael plenty of chances, but he wouldn't use his super strength for good. I hated when my scarecrows misbehaved. And if I got any more warnings from the Magic Council about my boys breaking out of their barns and scaring the locals, there'd be consequences.

"There must be a reason he keeps going walkabout, or rather, rampage about." I raised a light spell over my head, casting a pale glow to chase away the shadows in the forest. When I got back to the production barn, I'd run through each step I went through to bring my incredible scarecrows to life. I was certain I hadn't gotten anything wrong, but maybe I'd muddled the steps.

And a Grimsbane scarecrow couldn't afford to be muddled. I made the best scarecrows in the business, so my reputation was at stake. My workload felt never-ending, though, and I sometimes worked tired, which could cause problems like this.

Shamrock's large hand rested on my shoulder.

"Do you see something?" I whispered.

He moved in front of me and growled. My scarecrows didn't talk much, but I had a strong bond with Shamrock that enabled us to link thoughts and communicate telepathically. I trusted him to put my safety before anything else. And when he growled, I listened.

Shamrock stalked toward a patch of trees, and I took a moment to pull out a pouch of my powdered pumpkin and tipped the contents on my tongue. This was another talent of mine. Fresh pumpkins, magically enhanced scarecrows, and my secret powdered pumpkin. It went great with everything.

Buoyed by the energy giving properties of the powdered pumpkin, I continued tracking Michael's footprints. I squeaked as Shamrock lifted me off my feet and spun me around, using his back as a shield.

A second later, something heavy thudded against him.

I sparked orange magic on my fingers as I squirmed out of his grip. A large rock lay by Shamrock's feet, and when I examined his back, there was a dent in it.

"Michael, stop throwing things. We're trying to help." I raised my hand to allow the orange glow to light the trees. Several small pairs of eyes blinked at me for a second before vanishing among the foliage.

Shamrock growled again and punched away a huge branch that flew toward us.

"Come home and we can get you fixed," I said.

There was a rustle from nearby trees, and Shamrock took off running toward it.

I was right behind him, but had to dodge a large chestnut brown fox as it rocketed out of the shrubs. I almost lost my balance, but righted myself and kept running.

"Shamrock, don't hurt Michael. There's a chance we can help him." But it felt like a slim chance. Lately, I hadn't been on top of things. The farm was busy, the scarecrows were rambunctious, and my closest friends had recently gotten entangled in some puzzling mysteries that had distracted me. And then there was my ongoing search for Brodie.

Two heavy things colliding reached my ears, and I sped up. I glanced down to see the fox trotting beside me. "I suppose you think this is funny."

The fox glanced my way and kept running, his thick tail swishing from side to side.

"I would too if I saw a witch and her scarecrow sidekick chasing around the woods in the dead of night. You'd be wise to keep away from my boys, though. They're mean when they're angry." They could be mean most of the time, but that was how I made them. My scarecrows were the best bodyguards a magic user could wish for.

The fox slowed, but I kept running. I dove into the deep shadows of the forest without pausing. This wasn't the safest place to visit in the middle of the night, but I had my scarecrows as backup, when they weren't pounding each other to pieces. And there were dozens of them back at the farm. All I needed to do was whistle, and they'd come running.

They were the best protective army a witch could want. Although they came with a frustrating habit of chasing delivery people who came to my farm. But it was a small price to pay. And I loved my work. Even if it led me along a twisty, dangerous path at midnight to fix a small problem of my making.

I emerged into a clearing to see Michael just breaking free from Shamrock's headlock. He slammed his huge fist into Shamrock's chest and bolted away.

"Michael! This is your last warning. Come back to the barn with me now."

Michael didn't stop running.

I fired up my magic, regret simmering inside me. Michael was a failure, and it made me sad to extinguish one of my creations. With a heavy heart, I launched a powerful jet of bright orange magic at him. It slammed into Michael's back and sent him to the dirt.

I strode over, turning him with my foot, and pressed my hand against his chest where his heart should be. "I'm sorry, but you're out of control. Michael, it's time for you to sleep." I dragged out my life giving magic.

Michael struggled for a few seconds, twisting beneath my hand. But it was no use fighting. This was my magic, and I could give and take it easily.

A lump formed in my throat as the glow in his large eyes faded, and he returned to nothing more than a huge pile of straw, sticks, and baggy clothing.

Power tingled on my fingers before trickling up my arm and settling as a warm glow in my chest. It was a glow I'd always feel. It would remind me of Michael.

The fox appeared in the clearing and ambled over. It sniffed around what was left of Michael a few times, and then sat, curled its tail around its feet, and looked at me as if waiting for the next scene to begin.

I sat back on my heels and stared at the sky. "We've had two blood moons recently. They always make the magic in Witch Haven unstable."

The fox flicked its tail as if it wasn't sure it believed me.

A low warning growl rumbled behind me. There was a rush of air over my head as Shamrock launched at the fox.

I scrambled to my feet. "Shamrock, no! Let that fox go."

The fox was squirming in Shamrock's huge hands. It twisted around and sank its teeth into his arm.

Shamrock wouldn't feel the bite, but I'd be the one making repairs once we got home, so I needed to minimize the damage.

"No more fighting. We can all be friends."

The fox wriggled out of Shamrock's grasp, bounced against his chest, landed on me, and shot off.

I hit the dirt and sprawled on the ground as Shamrock bolted after the fox. As much as I loved my scarecrows, I sometimes wished they weren't so intent on killing everything they saw. But they'd always been like that. My scarecrows protected those they worked for. And they went to some impressive households. I'd even sent a troop of scarecrows to Windsor Castle to look after a member of the royal family.

I stared at the moon, taking a minute to get my breath back. I should do more investigation to see how badly these blood moons were affecting my boys. If things got any worse, I'd have to halt production. But with a six-month waiting list, and customers paying huge down payments to get their own custom-made killer scarecrow, the option to take a break wasn't there.

Rolling to my feet, I brushed off fox pawprints and took off after Shamrock.

When I thought about it, it sounded like I lived in a twisted fairytale. Twisted being the right word. Nothing was straightforward in Witch Haven, but I wouldn't have it any other way. I loved this tiny village. I had my friends around me and a thriving business. I had so many happy memories here. And a few tragic ones, too.

It was easy to follow the path Shamrock and the fox had taken. The smashed branches and trampled bushes showed me their route. Unfortunately, it was back toward the houses. People could be at risk if I didn't stop them.

I sped up and caught a glimpse of Shamrock. I whistled for him to come back. He ignored me. That was unusual. Shamrock was one of my more well-behaved scarecrows, and it wasn't like him to disobey a return command. That fox must have really annoyed him.

"Shamrock! If you don't behave, I'll take you to the stables, along with what's left of Michael. I know you hate the horses."

That made him slow. I never liked anything to go to waste, so the scarecrows who didn't turn out quite right were gathered up, and I took them to the local equine sanctuary. Hettie Crane was always grateful to have the extra straw, and the horses loved the pumpkin.

Reduce, reuse, recycle. That was a motto I lived by. And even if I was sad my failed scarecrows didn't get the long life I'd planned for them, the horses got a tasty feed.

I'd almost caught up with Shamrock and was about to give him a piece of my mind, when something with large black wings and a wicked sharp beak swooped from a branch, glinting talons aimed for my eyes. I fell to the ground and rolled, but not before the creature snared my hair in its talons.

"Hey, let go." My scalp burned as the feathered beast tried to take me with it.

The bird, which looked like a cross between a vulture and a Bald Eagle, squawked and kept beating its wings. Sharp feeling magic prickled off its talons as it struggled to restrain me.

"Quit yanking on my hair. I'm not a midnight snack." I reached up for the bird, getting a stab on the hand for my trouble. The forest was full of creatures like this, so it was only a matter of time before I encountered one. And it was just my luck that Shamrock was intent on destroying that innocent fox, rather than helping me.

I tried to get my fingers in my mouth to whistle for more scarecrows, but the bird critter was jerking me about so hard I could only make a pitiful hissy noise.

A warm whoosh of air blasted past me, and a second later, my feet hit the dirt. I crouched as I assessed the threat. "Oh! Sol. What are you doing here?"

Sol Vossen held the huge bird in a large, suntanned fist. He'd been working with me for almost five months, and I wasn't sure what I'd done before he joined the farm. He was hard working, steadfast, always turned up on time, never complained if I asked him to work overtime, and the scarecrows liked him.

"Odessa, are you hurt?" He strode over and caught hold of my elbow as he tossed the bird free. The bird cawed its unhappiness, but a glare from Sol sent it flapping away.

"I'm okay. More spooked than anything." My heart raced as Sol examined my head.

"That was a diamond griffin hybrid. It could have ripped your head clean off your shoulders. Are you sure you aren't injured?" His voice had a deep, reassuring rumble to it.

I patted my head, my fingers brushing his large, calloused palm. "I don't think so. It got its feet caught in my hair and didn't want to let go."

"It's their breeding season. It was probably looking for a meal for its young."

I chuckled. "I would have made some meal."

There was a glint of something I didn't recognize in Sol's eyes as his gaze flickered over me. But it was gone as soon as it arrived. "It's not a good idea to be in the forest on your own."

"I'm not alone. Shamrock's out here. We had a situation with Michael."

Concern crossed Sol's face. "He got out again?"

"He did."

"I thought we could bring him back, get him to focus." Sol lowered his hand, but remained close. I could smell the familiar scent of apple wood smoke and pumpkin he carried on him. The smell always made me relax and think of home.

"I've had to let him go. Michael was too difficult to handle." I smoothed down my hair. "I'm wondering if I'm losing my touch with the scarecrows."

"You could never do that. It's what you're known for."

It was rare I doubted myself, but standing here with a stinging scalp and a recently deceased scarecrow on my hands, it made a woman wonder.

"Odessa, you can't save them all. Some scarecrows are simply too intense."

"My magic makes them that way." I shook out my hands. Was I the problem? Was it time to do things differently?

Everyone needed to evaluate their lives and figure out when it was time to change things up. I was a third of the way through my life, so I was maybe due for an early midlife crisis. People wouldn't think it weird if I slid off the rails. After all, things hadn't gone how I'd planned them. There should be children in the farmhouse by now, and I should be happily married to Brodie.

Sol's gentle sigh knocked me from my early midlife crisis musings. "Is there anything I can help you with?"

"You can help me stop Shamrock. If he goes running through the neighbors' backyards again, someone will report him to the Magic Council. I can't lose him, too. Shamrock is special."

Sol stepped back and nodded. "Then let's go find Shamrock."

It took twenty minutes of tracking before we found him. He was hunkered down by a large outbuilding in the back of Raina and Alastair Chalice's large, neatly manicured back yard. Well, it had been manicured, but it looked like the fox and Shamrock had led a merry dance around the lawn a few times.

"Shamrock, get your straw-filled butt over here," I hiss-whispered. "And leave that fox alone. You'd better not have eaten him."

Shamrock looked my way, then glared at the base of the outbuilding.

"I'm not playing around." I raised a warning blast of magic.

He didn't move. Stubborn scarecrow. But then I made him that way, so I only had myself to blame.

"Shamrock! I've had enough for one night, and I'd have been in trouble if Sol hadn't been here to help." I glanced at Sol. "What were you doing in the woods so late?"

"Looking for moonflowers. I was making a tincture for my shoulder, and they're more powerful when the moon is full."

"Your shoulder is still troubling you?" He'd pulled it when dealing with three angry scarecrows who wouldn't behave.

Sol rolled the joint and gave me an easy smile. "It's getting better."

I went to touch his shoulder, but Shamrock suddenly loomed next to me, a sullen look on his face. He clutched my arm and moved me away from Sol.

"Stop. You know Sol is safe. And he just saved me from a diamond griffin. That should have been your job."

A humming noise filled my head as Shamrock formed a mind link with me.

"Sorry. Bad fox." Shamrock's voice was a jumble of growls and tweets mixed in with the words.

"No, just a curious fox."

"You hurt?"

"I'm fine, thanks to Sol." I nodded at Sol. I should give him more responsibility on the farm. He hadn't put a foot wrong since he'd started working for me. It was time I rewarded him.

I returned Sol's warm smile. I could find him a girlfriend. He hadn't mentioned anyone special, but he was an attractive man if you liked the large, cuddly teddy bear type. And who didn't like a beefy guy to squeeze you tight on a cold night?

"Shamrock, go find what's left of Michael and take him to the farm," I said. "Then get yourself in the barn and rest."

His gaze shot to the outbuilding, and his menacing growl filled my head.

"No! No more foxes. Foxes are our friends. They deserve to live just as much as we do."

Shamrock stamped his foot before marching back toward the forest.

Sol chuckled as he crossed his arms over his broad chest. "I've never seen anyone handle scarecrows the way you do. It never ceases to amaze me."

I wriggled my fingers, and magic sparkled on the ends of them. "As you said, it's what I do. Now, how about we—"

"Odessa Grimsbane! What are you doing in my yard?" Raina Chalice stood by the open back door of the house, dressed in a dark green set of pajamas.

"Sorry to disturb you, Raina. We were out for a late-night stroll, when I thought I saw someone in your yard. I wanted to make sure no one was stealing." It sounded a convincing lie to me, although I wasn't sure how I'd explain the messed up lawn if she noticed it.

Raina arched an eyebrow, her approving gaze moving over Sol. "I thought you two had snuck in here for a sneaky canoodle."

I burst out laughing. "Don't be silly. I'm not single." My fingers went to my empty wedding ring finger.

Sol sucked in a breath, and his gaze cut to me. "I should make sure Shamrock's behaving himself. Or I could stay. Walk you back."

"No. I'll be fine. Thanks for tonight. I'd have been in a mess if you weren't here to help." I patted his arm.

"Anytime. I'm always here for you." He nodded a good night to Raina and me before striding away.

I walked over to Raina. She was a well put together woman in her mid-fifties with short dark hair and intense green eyes. "I didn't mean to wake you."

Raina's gaze shifted from Sol to me. "You're fine. I hadn't gone to bed. I've been having trouble sleeping lately, so I was making a hot drink and thought I'd sit up and read."

"You're not sleeping? Are you worried about something?"

"Well, I have been having a few problems recently." Raina clenched her hands so tight I could see the white of her knuckles beneath her skin.

"Is there anything I can help with?"

She shook her head. "Only if you know how to deal with an unhappy ghost who doesn't want to move on."

I grinned at her. "Ghost hunting is a hobby of mine."

Raina's eyes widened. "Are you being serious?"

"Of course. Are you sure it's a haunting, though?" My stomach fluttered with hope. Could this be the ghost I'd been searching for?

"Yes. Absolutely." Raina bit her lip and glanced over her shoulder. "I'm getting desperate and don't know what to do. Have you got time to come in now?"

"Um... sure. I was going home, but I've got time."

"You're an angel. The ghost has been active all evening, and I don't know what to do to make him happy." Raina ushered me inside.

So, it was a male ghost. This sounded promising. "I'd be happy to help. Lead the way and introduce me to your ghost friend." And maybe, just maybe, I'd finally find my lost ghost and have my missing piece back.

Hauntings and High Jinx is available in e-book and paperback
ISBN: 978-1-915378-34-7